ONE WRONG MOVE

If he hadn't taken the next three steps, Fargo wouldn't have been able to guess what Ollie had in mind. But the way he moved, the way his back was arched unnaturally, told Fargo what Ollie intended.

Fortunately for Fargo, Ollie was not only obvious about trying to hide a gun down the back of his Levi's; he was also so hotheaded he couldn't wait for a good chance to use it.

Ollie shouted, "Now!" and flung himself to the ground. In some ways the moment was pathetic. He had trouble ripping the gun from the back of his jeans, and by the time it saw daylight Fargo had put a bullet straight into the top of Ollie's skull. Blood and brain exploded like a fireworks display. . . .

THE
TRAILSMAN
#323

WYOMING
DEATH TRAP

by

Jon Sharpe

A SIGNET BOOK

SIGNET
Published by New American Library, a division of
Penguin Group (USA) Inc., 375 Hudson Street,
New York, New York 10014, USA
Penguin Group (Canada), 90 Eglinton Avenue East, Suite 700, Toronto,
Ontario M4P 2Y3, Canada (a division of Pearson Penguin Canada Inc.)
Penguin Books Ltd., 80 Strand, London WC2R 0RL, England
Penguin Ireland, 25 St. Stephen's Green, Dublin 2,
Ireland (a division of Penguin Books Ltd.)
Penguin Group (Australia), 250 Camberwell Road, Camberwell, Victoria 3124,
Australia (a division of Pearson Australia Group Pty. Ltd.)
Penguin Books India Pvt. Ltd., 11 Community Centre, Panchsheel Park,
New Delhi - 110 017, India
Penguin Group (NZ), 67 Apollo Drive, Rosedale, North Shore 0632,
New Zealand (a division of Pearson New Zealand Ltd.)
Penguin Books (South Africa) (Pty.) Ltd., 24 Sturdee Avenue,
Rosebank, Johannesburg 2196, South Africa

Penguin Books Ltd., Registered Offices:
80 Strand, London WC2R 0RL, England

First published by Signet, an imprint of New American Library,
a division of Penguin Group (USA) Inc.

First Printing, September 2008
10 9 8 7 6 5 4 3 2 1

The first chapter of this book previously appeared in *Apache Ambush*, the
three hundred twenty-second volume in this series.

The Trailsman

Beginnings . . . they bend the tree and they mark the man. Skye Fargo was born when he was eighteen. Terror was his midwife, vengeance his first cry. Killing spawned Skye Fargo, ruthless, cold-blooded murder. Out of the acrid smoke of gunpowder still hanging in the air, he rose, cried out a promise never forgotten.

The Trailsman they began to call him all across the West: searcher, scout, hunter, the man who could see where others only looked, his skills for hire but not his soul, the man who lived each day to the fullest, yet trailed each tomorrow. Skye Fargo, the Trailsman, the seeker who could take the wildness of a land and the wanting of a woman and make them his own.

Wyoming Country, 1861—
sometimes you don't know who to trust,
and you find yourself trapped in a deadly game.

1

Something was wrong.

Skye Fargo came through the narrow mountain pass and looked below to the stage station sprawled across a small, rocky stretch of land. On a fine, sunny morning in Wyoming, a stage pulled up in front of the place. There should have been some sign of activity. Even the horses in the rope corral seemed strangely still and quiet. The few scattered outbuildings cast deep morning shadows.

Fargo's lake blue eyes narrowed as he sat his Ovaro stallion and scanned the situation more carefully. For the past two months he'd been working for a Mr. Andrew Lund, the wealthiest man in this part of the Territory. Not only did Lund own the two largest gold mines, he also owned the largest stagecoach line. Fargo's job was to travel the trouble routes and see if he could stop the robbers who'd been making Lund's life hell. Fargo had been forced to do some killing, but so far there had been significant improvement in the safety of the routes. His biggest regret was that despite his efforts, two drivers and a passenger had been killed in one part of the Territory while Fargo had been pulled away to sack a gang in the other.

Fargo knew the man and wife who ran this station for Lund. They were in their sixties, had been farmers until they got too old and too weary to fight off Indians any longer, and ran the cleanest station with the best food anywhere in the entire Lund organization.

Whatever the problem was, it wasn't Indians. Indians weren't quiet unless they were lying in wait. Plus, one of the Indians would have been rounding up the horses in the corral, running them off if not stealing them.

To the west of the station was a line of scrub pine. At the moment a couple of deer were sampling the grass carpeting the thin area of forest.

Fargo walked his Ovaro over to the trees, hiding it in a separate copse of pines. He ran to the denser spread of trees and began working his way in morning shadow to the area behind the station. The scent of pine was sweet and the forest creatures inquisitive as this giant made his way through their kingdom.

Nothing moved in back of the adobe-sided station, either. Empty crates were stacked on one side of the rear door; the other side was empty. There was a window on the empty side.

Fargo moved carefully, crouching down, Colt drawn and ready, working his way to the window on the back wall. The only sounds were those of the soughing mountain winds, the cries of a soaring hawk, and the creaking of pine limbs when the wind came hard.

He ducked below the window, preparing himself for surprise. He might well ease himself up to peer inside and find himself staring at another human being. A damned unfriendly one.

He inched himself up to the window. No face awaited him. What he saw was self-explanatory. In the center of the station four passengers stood together while three masked gunmen went through their bags. A fourth gunman stood to the side, holding a sawed-off shotgun on them.

Fargo didn't see Lem Cantwell, the station manager, at first, but as his eyes searched the large central room inside they spotted a snakelike line of red on the stone floor and traced the line all the way to the bloody white-haired head of an older man. With a dark ragged hole the size of a baseball on the left side of his head, there was no doubt that he was dead. Fargo didn't see Pauline, Lem's wife. Had the bastards killed her, too?

The first thing he had to do was check his anger. Much as he wanted to go bursting in there now, he'd probably only get himself killed and help nobody.

He forced himself to focus on the job at hand and not on the Cantwells.

He crouched down again and duckwalked over to the side of the door. He stood up, slid his hand over to the doorknob, and gently began turning it back and forth.

The conversation inside went on without interruption. One of the passengers was a pretty girl and so naturally at least two of the bastards were talking about how they were going to rape her when they were done robbing everybody. A third robber kept threatening the passengers to turn over everything valuable they had on them. He said that anybody caught holding out would be killed. But surely by now the passengers knew that they were to be killed no matter what they said or did.

Nobody had heard Fargo twisting the doorknob back and forth.

He twisted faster, harder, until one of them said: "What the hell's that?"

By now the girl was crying so hard that hearing the doorknob turn was even more difficult. But between her sobs one of the men said, "It's the back door."

"The back door?" another robber said. "Who the hell'd be coming in the back door?" Then: "Lou, you go find out."

"Cover me," Lou said. "This is strange."

Fargo gave the knob a final twist. Then he pressed himself flat against the adobe and waited. The chinking sound of Lou's spurs grew louder the closer he got to the door.

Fargo knew he had only seconds to act.

The door opened, and the brim of a filthy white Stetson poked out of the doorframe. Fargo slapped the hat off Lou's head and just as Lou turned to see

3

who his assailant was—bringing his gun up—Fargo brought his own revolver down so hard on Lou's skull that the scrawny man dropped without another sound. Fargo started dragging him away just as he hit the ground.

Fargo knew that the men inside still had the advantage. Three of them plus a sawed-off shotgun. If he went in there and started shooting, he'd do the very thing he hoped to avoid—get the passengers killed.

He heard shouts and threats, and then a couple of the men running to the back door.

But Fargo was still dragging Lou by his long, filthy black hair. Lou was going to have one hell of a headache when he woke up.

On the side of the station Fargo found an empty barrel. He hauled Lou and the barrel in front of the building. By now Lou was conscious, spluttering and cursing. Fargo put his gun to Lou's right temple and said, "Turn the barrel over so you can sit on it and then sit down."

"What the hell you think you're doing? And why the hell'd you have to drag me by my hair, you son of a bitch? You know how much my head hurts?"

Fargo ripped the man's mask off. He was a middle-aged man, with pinched features, a broken nose, a brown walleye on the left. "What's your name?"

The man said nothing. Fargo slapped him hard across the back of the head. "You hear me? What's your name?"

"Clemmons."

"Any of the others named Clemmons?"

Silence again. This time Fargo grabbed a handful of hair and pulled. Clemmons' scream played off the mountains.

Clemmons said, "They're all my brothers."

"I was hoping for that." These days many outlaw gangs were kin of some sort. "Brothers" was the jackpot.

Fargo shouted, "You heard him scream. The next

4

time he screams it'll be because I put a bullet through his head. You want your brother to die?"

The expected response: "You hurt my brother, mister, you're as good as dead."

"That may be, but brother Lou here'll die before I do."

"Help us!" cried one of the passengers.

"I'll tell you how this is going to work," Fargo shouted. The front of the station had a wide door in the center and a small window on the south end. There was no face in the window. "I'm going to give you one minute to let the passengers go. If they don't start coming out, I kill your brother."

"Then we'll kill them."

"Fine. But your brother dies with them."

"He'll kill me, Sam! You don't know him! He already tore out half my hair draggin' me around here!"

"Help us!" the same passenger cried again.

"I want Pauline Cantwell, too."

"If you mean the old woman, she's dead."

Fargo was tempted to kill Lou Clemmons here and now. The Clemmonses would occupy a special place in any hell Fargo designed. But the purpose of using Lou as a hostage was to get the passengers out safe. It was a gamble, Fargo knew. The men inside might just kill them all right now. But they planned to kill them anyway. At least this way there was a chance they'd survive.

"The old lady's dead, just like you're gonna be."

"Goddamn, Sam! Don't make him no madder than he already is!" Lou Clemmons pleaded.

"I'm counting off starting right now, Clemmons. If you don't send them out right away, you'll be burying your brother this morning."

"Listen to him, Sam! Listen to him!"

Fargo could hear them talking. Arguing, really. Finally a new voice shouted: "Don't kill him!"

"Then send out the passengers."

"You son of a bitch," one of them said.

"That won't get you anywhere. Now open the door and send them out."

Fargo's nose detected a warm sour smell. Lou Clemmons had wet himself. "This isn't right, mister. You'd be killing me in cold blood."

"How'd the Cantwells die in there? I should've killed you already."

Clemmons sucked up tears.

"Ten seconds!" Fargo shouted.

Heavy footsteps inside. Arguing again. The door was pulled back.

A man in a Roman collar and a dark suit came out first. The suit had been splashed with his own vomit. When he reached the ground outside, he flung his arms to the heavens and offered a silent prayer. Then he stumbled toward Fargo.

The second person out was a heavyset woman in a shawl and a gingham dress. She had a hard prairie face. She looked a lot tougher than the minister and, for that matter, Lou Clemmons. She walked straight for Fargo and took her place standing behind him where the minister was. Fargo wondered uncharitably if the minister would faint.

The girl came third. She wore brown butternuts and a white cotton blouse that hung in shreds. They'd already started to assault her. She didn't seem to notice or care that one of her fine small breasts was exposed. She was dazed and lost. The heavyset woman walked to her, took off her shawl, and wrapped it around the girl to cover her. She slid her arm around her and then half carried her to a position behind Fargo.

Last came a little elderly man whose face was covered in blood. What the hell had a little old man said or done to them that caused him to be beaten so severely? His face was a pudding of red blood under which small features could dimly be seen. He wore a green suit soaked with his own gore, and the way he stumbled, Fargo wondered if he could even make it to a position behind him.

The minister hurried to him. He literally picked up

the small man in his arms and rushed him back to where the woman and the girl stood. He set him down and immediately began wiping the old man's face with a cloth and soothing him with words. Fargo thought much better of the religious man now.

"Now we want our brother, you bastard!"

"Not going to get him," Fargo said. He angled his head quickly so that the four behind him could hear. "Head for those trees over there. Get way out of range."

"Oh, shit," Lou Clemmons said, and just after he spoke the words he filled his pants.

"Hurry," Fargo snapped to the four.

He didn't watch them but he heard them walking, running, dragging, scurrying to get out of range any way they could. Now it was just Fargo and the Clemmonses.

"We want our brother. Send him over here."

Fargo pretended not to hear. "I want all three of you to walk out here and throw your guns down. You don't do that, your brother dies right now."

"That ain't what you promised."

"I didn't promise anything. Now do like I say or he's dead."

"Please, Sam! Please!" Lou Clemmons didn't mind fouling himself, apparently, but crying was so unmanly he worked hard at pretending those weren't tears running down his cheeks or trembling in his voice.

"All right. We're coming out."

"One step outside, you throw your guns away or he dies."

"I'm getting goddamned sick of you."

"Feeling's mutual. Now do like I say."

The door squeaked open and two men who had the misfortune of looking pretty much like their brother Lou came out. They'd tossed their masks. There was no point now.

"The guns," Fargo said.

"You're gonna be dead in three minutes."

"Sam, Sam, please don't say that to him," Clemmons whined. "Shit's sake man, he's got a gun barrel pressed right against my temple."

"The guns."

They sneered and they stalled, but when they heard the hammer pulled back on Fargo's Colt they pitched their guns a few feet away.

Sun glinted off something metal. Fargo angled his head so he could follow the brightness. A rifle barrel was edging its way into the front window.

"Tell the other one to get out here."

"Sam, Sam, tell Ollie. Tell him he's gonna get me killed."

From inside Ollie bellowed: "I can get a clean shot at him like I said, Sam! I just bust the window and kill him! I got me a rifle!"

"Tell him to get his ass out here. Time the window's broken, you got a dead brother on your hands."

Sam frowned. Fargo figured he'd probably gone along with the idea of suddenly showing a rifle and gunning him down. But now that Sam and his other brother were out here it looked different. Killing Fargo from the window now looked hopeless.

"Get your ass out here like the man says, Ollie."

"But I got a rifle."

"Yeah, and this man's got Lou. Now get your ass out here. I don't want to tell you again."

"Damn you, Sam." Ollie sounded like a very disappointed child. He made a lot of noise slamming against things as he crossed the length of the station to the front door. He stood in the doorway, another Lou Clemmons look-alike except for the meanness quotient. The good Lord must have filled up his meanness tank full to the brim. "I shoulda let him kill you, Lou. Lettin' him snag you the way he done."

"Just get out here so he'll let me go," Clemmons said.

Ollie spat some of his chaw to the ground and then started walking his way to the others. He walked slowly, hoping to irritate Fargo and show everybody he wasn't afraid. Like too many gunnies, he was a ham actor.

"Pitch the rifle."

"Yessir, Commander, sir. I sure wouldn't want to displease you none." He spat again but he pitched the rifle.

If he hadn't taken the next three steps, Fargo wouldn't have been able to guess what Ollie had in mind. But the way he moved, the way his back was arched unnaturally, told Fargo what Ollie intended.

Fortunately for Fargo, Ollie was not only obvious about trying to hide a gun down the back of his Levi's, he was also so hotheaded he couldn't wait for a good chance to use it.

Ollie shouted, "Now!" and flung himself down to the ground. In some ways the moment was pathetic. He had trouble ripping the gun from the back of his jeans, and by the time it saw daylight Fargo had put a bullet straight into the top of Ollie's skull. Blood and brain exploded like a fireworks display.

Fargo had been distracted long enough for the other two to grab their guns. Lou Clemmons screamed, "No! Please, no!" Those were his last earthly words. His brothers, attempting to shoot Fargo, killed their brother instead. He fell sideways off the barrel.

By this time Fargo had thrown himself to the ground with a good deal more success than Ollie had. He rolled left, he rolled right, with enough speed to make hitting him difficult. Their shots came in gun-emptying barrages. Rage had made them forget that they had only six bullets apiece, maybe fewer unless they'd reloaded inside.

Fargo shot with more care than either of the remaining brothers. He got Sam in the throat. The man went dramatically, calling out for his mother before he fell to the ground.

The other brother he got twice in the heart. The man's gun went flying into the air. Then he pitched forward, slamming his head on a razor-sharp edge of

9

embedded rock. The fall probably would have killed him without the bullets.

Fargo glanced at Lou Clemmons. He'd been shot twice in the face. He was as much of a mess as station manager Lem Cantwell was inside.

Fargo got to his feet. For long seconds all he could hear were the echoes of all the gunfire; all he could smell and taste was gun smoke. But then the wind came and cleansed the air of the gun smoke, and birds replaced the crack of bullets.

He turned to the people he'd ordered out of range. The killings inside the station and out had dulled their eyes and crippled their bodies. They watched him suspiciously, as if he might turn on them, as if this might be a nightmare without end.

But he smiled at them. The heavyset woman, who clutched the girl as if she were her daughter, laughed and said: "It's really over, isn't it?"

"Yeah," Fargo said, "it's really over."

2

The Negro waiter said, "Here is your drink, Mr. Fargo."

The white-jacketed servant offered Fargo a small tray. Fargo took his glass of bourbon and water and thanked the man. "Is this the biggest party you've ever seen here?"

"Just about. And the people keep coming."

The occasion was Andrew Lund's fifty-seventh birthday, and it was being held in the finest, shiniest, most imposing mansion Fargo had ever been inside. He stood beneath a chandelier so vast and so bright it could light the countryside. To his right an enormous staircase was pitched at such a steep angle it promised to lead all the way to heaven. From the ballroom came the strains of a dance orchestra. And everywhere, in and out of various rooms, floated men and women in formal evening clothes, the richest and most powerful people in the Territory. If you didn't believe they were the richest and most powerful, Fargo had noted, just listen to them talk. They'd assure you of that fact in time.

Fargo's only concession to fancy dressing was his white starched shirt, black trousers, and shined black boots. He'd had his long hair trimmed and his growth of beard shaved. Though he worked for Lund, he had no idea why Lund would invite him to his birthday party.

Just then Lund appeared. He was a tall man,

powerful-looking despite his years. He had worked as everything from a stevedore to a ranch hand before making one of the biggest gold strikes in the Territory several years ago. Even in his evening clothes and white hair there was a rawboned quality to his manner.

"Well, Fargo, you look just as uncomfortable as I thought you would." Lund laughed.

"You invited me here to torture me, huh?"

Lund was about to say something when a striking young blond woman came up to him and touched his arm. Her low-cut blue taffeta dress revealed a rich body at its youthful peak. She had an attractive face with a wry smile and intelligent blue eyes.

"I was hoping you'd introduce me, Dad," she said, smiling at Fargo. "This handsome man's the only one anywhere near my age here tonight."

Lund slid his arm around his daughter and said, "My favorite child, Fargo."

"His only child. He never adds that."

"My favorite and only child. Serena."

"Glad to meet you, Serena."

Lund laughed. "And I know why she wants to meet you, too, Fargo."

"Do you dance, Mr. Fargo?" Serena asked.

"Only when somebody's shooting bullets at my feet."

She had a girlish laugh Fargo liked. "So far tonight I've had my feet trod on, my bottom grabbed two or three times by lechers older than my father, and two proposals of marriage from men so drunk they apparently forgot that they were *already* married."

"She's going to drag you out on that dance floor one way or the other, Fargo. You may as well resign yourself to that. Between my wife, Alexis, and my daughter, I don't stand a chance of making any decisions on my own."

Fargo noticed a distinct look of displeasure on Serena's face when the subject of Alexis came up. Her stepmother couldn't be much older than Serena herself.

"So what will it be, Mr. Fargo? Will you come willingly to the ballroom or will I have to get tough with you?"

Lund clapped Fargo on the back. "I've been telling everybody tonight about what you did at that stage station. The lives you saved. Everybody here's afraid of you, Fargo."

"Except me," Serena said. "I'm just as fierce as you are, Mr. Fargo, when it comes to looking for dancing partners."

Lund leaned in to Fargo and whispered, "I need to talk some business later on tonight. We'll go into my study."

"I heard the word 'business,' Dad. Can't you relax for one night? The night of your birthday?"

Lund laughed. "I warned you, Fargo. She's nobody to trifle with. One way or the other she gets her way."

They watched as he made his way to another group of drinkers and talkers, all this played out beneath the chandelier that burned like a heavenly body. Among all the dark evening clothes passed Negro waiters in white jackets and maids in gray dresses serving people used to being served, people used to being obeyed.

Just then a young woman who looked uncomfortable in her blue organdy gown walked toward them. She wasn't exactly pretty, but in a very proper kid-sister way there was a curious sexuality in the thin, pale body and the somewhat prudish face.

"Good evening, Delia," Serena said.

"Good evening, Serena."

That neither woman cared much for the other was obvious in their tones. Forced. Very forced. Delia nodded to Fargo. She didn't seem any happier to see him than she was to see Serena.

When she'd passed by, Serena said, "Delia Powell. She's Alexis' personal maid. Came with Alexis from the East."

"I gather you're not the best of friends."

"Is it that obvious?"

"Afraid so."

She considered her words before she spoke. "Delia is Alexis' best friend. There are times when Delia doesn't want to have anything to do with me. She didn't like me from the moment she saw me."

Fargo wondered if the same wasn't true for her. It was a case of daughter and wife competing for the attention and affection of Lund. And the personal maid always taking the side of the woman she served.

Then Serena changed the subject. "But you don't want to hear all that." She put on her most ingratiating and very seductive smile. "My father can't stop talking about what you did at that stage station."

"He makes too much of it."

"Sure he does, Mr. Fargo. One man up against four. Happens every day." She slid a slender arm through his. Her perfume dazzled his senses. "But if you're brave enough to do that, you should be brave enough to dance with me. I promise I'll protect you."

He smiled. He liked her, the soft swell of her breasts, the playful hint of her blue eyes, and the sly, little-girl smile.

"Well, I guess it'll be all right. I don't know anybody here so when I make a fool of myself nobody'll know who I am."

"Not the way my father's been bragging about you, I'm afraid. *Everybody* knows who you are."

"You just *had* to tell me that, didn't you?"

She giggled and poked him in the ribs. "Uh-huh. Now let's go to the ballroom."

Fargo knew mountain dancing and square dancing. Not as a participant but as an observer. He had no idea what he was observing here, five minutes after they'd entered the ballroom where, under four small chandeliers, elegant ladies and gentlemen coupled, parted, and coupled again, all in rigid formations according to rules Fargo couldn't even guess at.

"I'm going to spare us both and not go out on that dance floor."

"A man who stood up to four gunmen and he's afraid to do a little dancing?"

"I'd rather go up against four gunmen any day," Fargo said. Then his attention was distracted. "There's your stepmother."

There were several beautiful women on the dance floor but none compelled the eye the way Alexis Lund did. Her dark beauty, a face so finely boned it resembled sculpture, and the slender, elegant body of the ballerina she'd been back in New York made looking away from her just about impossible. The eye just wasn't accustomed to a woman of such exquisite looks. She was twenty-nine years old.

"Oh, God," Serena said as she watched a blond man approach Alexis in the center of the floor. He was one of those men who just escaped being pretty. His slight swagger told Fargo that nobody on earth could be quite as pleased with himself as this man. "One of Dad's business partners in freighting," Serena said. "Brett Norton. He inherited several businesses from his father. He likes to sleep around with married women."

"That can be a dangerous business."

"I think that's the part of it he likes. Dad detests him. He's tried to buy him out several times."

"Looks like your stepmother doesn't mind him."

Serena took his hand. "I'd better not say any more about that. Now come on. I'm going to teach you the two-step."

"The what?"

Serena smiled. "You'll see."

And he did see. For the next fifteen minutes they practiced dancing in a dark recess of a hallway. When people passed by they looked greatly amused. Fargo towered over the small girl. He caught on to the two-step to a certain degree but when she suggested that he was ready for the ballroom he still moved around with the grace of a buffalo.

No matter how earnestly she tried to drag him into the center of the dancers, he stayed in a relatively shadowy corner of the huge room. Even so, a number of people smirked at them as they danced by the couple.

"This is going to ruin your reputation."

"My reputation's already ruined, Skye. I'm the 'spoiled, willful daughter' you read about in romance novels. The one who always loses the hero at the end of the book. The plucky poor girl always wins him." She glanced over at her stepmother. A short man with glossy black hair and a beard now danced with Alexis. He appeared to be comfortable in his fancy black evening suit with the brocaded plum-colored vest.

Fargo saw where Serena was looking and said, "At least he doesn't look as arrogant as the last one."

"James Holmes. He and Dad own the largest bank in the Territory together. I actually feel a little bit sorry for him. I found a letter he wrote to Alexis. He told her that he was in love with her and would leave his wife and children for her anytime she asked. I took it to Alexis. She'd left it on a small table in the hall outside the master bedroom. She can be very reckless. I told her that if I ever found out that she'd cheated on my father, I'd tell him immediately."

"What did she say about it?"

"Just shook her head. Said he was just having an infatuation and that she'd done nothing to encourage it. She said that she loved my father very much and would never be unfaithful to him."

"And you didn't believe her?"

A sweet smile. "Spoiled, willful daughters are very cynical people, Skye. I wired the Pinkertons in Denver. I told them that I wanted her investigated. They contacted their office in New York and two men there went to work making up a file on her." The music ended. "Why don't we get a drink and sit at one of those little tables? I'll have the punch."

As Fargo walked to the bar at the east end of the ballroom, he felt someone watching him. He turned his head slightly and met the gaze of Alexis Lund. Her full, soft lips parted in a half smile. She favored him with an almost imperceptible nod. Apparently the queen herself approved of him.

When he brought their drinks back and sat down, Serena said, "I saw that little smile Alexis gave you."

"Guess I didn't notice that."

"Sure you didn't." She touched the rim of her glass to her mouth and said, "Thank you for getting me my drink, kind sir."

"My pleasure."

The orchestra began playing again. Dancers filled the floor.

"I'm surprised you aren't more anxious to hear what the Pinkertons found out about my lovely step-mother."

"I figured you'd tell me when you were ready to."

"I'm ready." She sipped her punch and set her glass down. "Among other things, Alexis was married before. A rich older man who lost all his money through a very foolish investment. He became very sick. She walked out on him, took up with an actor."

"Maybe there are two sides to that story. Maybe the rich man wasn't exactly what he claimed to be, either. Maybe he beat her or something."

"Maybe. But I'm not done making my case. The next thing she did, after her affair with the actor, was take up with another rich older man. She was all set to marry him when his three children came to her and offered her a large amount of money to disappear. I'm sure they were thinking of their inheritance but I'm also sure they cared about their father and saw what she was. She took the money and vanished. She spent a year in London and Paris where she got involved with a wealthy married man. This time it was his wife who paid her off to go away."

"She must have a lot of her own money stashed away somewhere."

"That's the thing. She's terrible with money. Spends and spends and spends. Even my father complains

17

about her trips to Denver and St. Louis. Huge bills for clothes and furniture and traveling. So I doubt she has any of it left."

"I'm surprised a man in your dad's position didn't have her checked out the way you did."

She frowned. "I'd never seen him that way. The way he was with her. I suppose I resented it because I'd never seen him that way with my mother. And I was jealous of Alexis myself. I'll admit it. He wouldn't have her background checked because he was afraid they'd find something and that would spoil the illusion he has of her. That's what *I* think, anyway. I know his brother in Cincinnati wrote him a letter suggesting that, but my father just scoffed and called his brother an old woman." Then she said: "I could never tell my father what the detectives found out. He'd hate me forever. I love him too much to hurt him that way." She slid a gentle hand over his. "But you could. He'd listen to you and he wouldn't hate you for telling him."

So that was it. The quiet seduction he'd been enjoying. The sweet, fresh earnestness of the young woman. All to help persuade him that he should tell her father the truth about his wife.

"I can't help you, Serena. This isn't any of my business. This is a family matter."

She smiled. "I guess I'm not as charming as I thought."

"You're very charming and you know it. But this is between you and your father."

"And Alexis."

"And Alexis."

"I suppose you hate me now. Trying to use you. When I went to school back East they said that when you came right down to it, all a woman has is her charm." She touched his hand again. "I did my best. And I really do want to help my father."

Fargo followed the sudden track of her gaze. Whispers circulated throughout the ballroom as beneath the center chandelier Lund and Alexis came together.

The orchestra struck up a waltz and the couple began to dance. All the onlookers applauded. Lund and Alexis were the only dancers. Fargo was starting to tire of all the wealth and pomposity of the evening. He wanted back in his own duds with a beer in one hand and a cheroot in the other. He wouldn't mind taking Serena along for a night in his hotel room, but he reckoned that she wasn't used to that type of experience.

But as he looked closer at the couple he noticed how rigid their bodies were. Both of them were angled back at their waists, as if they didn't want to get closer. Their smiles were rigid, too.

"She's happy," Serena said. "The center of attention."

Fargo wished Lund hadn't told him to stay around. He wanted to get on his Ovaro and head back to town. The dance went on for a long time. About half-way through, other dancers took to the floor. All Fargo could see of the couple was Lund's white hair above the heads of the others.

"I think I'll go outside and have a smoke. I need a little air."

"I'm sorry if I made you mad." She was so winsome and erotic at that moment that Fargo wanted to grab her up and haul her off to the first private room they could find.

But proper folks probably didn't act that way. But then he'd never been proper.

"I'll be back," he said.

In the massive front doorway people stood smoking and talking. A good number of them were drunk and jovial. A woman slapped a man and he slapped her right back. The people around them found this greatly amusing.

Fargo found a side door that led to a small, deserted stone patio. He leaned against the wall and rolled himself a smoke and took in the gleam of the snow-peaked mountaintops in the moonlight. The air was clean, vital here. To hell with them inside. He didn't belong here and regretted that he'd come. Except for meeting Serena. She was a girl-woman, not quite grown up, but she was a damned appealing girl-woman.

He heard private coaches and surreys clatter up to the wide front steps of the mansion. People were starting to depart for the night. Inside, two choruses of a birthday song were being sung. Lund spoke for a few minutes afterward. Then there was applause and the orchestra began playing again.

Fargo looked east to the boomtown of Reliance. For all his civilized ways, Lund didn't seem to see anything wrong with the town he'd built remaining wild and generally lawless. It hadn't taken Fargo long to see that the sheriff and his deputies catered to the rich and the Lord help everybody else. Three or four times Fargo had stopped a deputy from pounding on a drunken miner with his billy club. The miners were harmlessly drunk and staggering their way home. Fargo would be drunk most of the time, too, if he had to work in mines that were subject to cave-ins, and, even worse, the possibility of running into veins of water—sometimes the exploding water was scalding and killed a man instantly. No, not a job Fargo would care to have, especially not for the wages paid and the galling evidence of so much wealth made on the backs of the workers. He'd actually seen a carriage trimmed in gold plying the main street the other day.

Fargo rolled another cigarette and thought about going back inside. He wished he knew where the study was. He'd go straight there rather than mingle with the people in the enormous vestibule.

But a voice said, "There you are, Fargo. I guess we can talk out here if we keep our voices low."

Lund's demeanor had changed from that of a man celebrating his birthday with friends to a man both anxious and angry. A small tic had developed under his left eye. Whatever was bothering him was bothering him a great deal.

Fargo leaned against the stone railing. "I take it something's come up with the stage line again."

He noticed that Lund's right hand made a fist. A big, tight one. "I wish it was as simple as that. This is personal, Fargo."

"Personal?"

"Yes," Lund said, his jaw muscles jutting, his fist white-knuckled now. "I believe my wife is seeing somebody on the side and I want you to start following her for me."

A laugh from a stone path not far away chastened him. "Maybe we'd better go to my study after all."

3

Leather couches and furnishings; book-lined walls; a framed photograph of Lund standing in work clothes outside his first mine; an outsize globe on a stand; and a desk clean and broad enough to play croquet on. The rich oak walls gleamed with the colors cast by the flames in the stone fireplace. And beyond the mullioned windows, framed exactly, were two of the highest snow-covered peaks, silver in the moonlight. This was a sanctuary, a place to shut away the world and relax. But given Lund's grief and anger the air was as tense as that of a saloon before a gunfight.

He got each of them brandies. He paced and talked. Fargo sat and listened.

"I can't be sure of it. But I have my suspicions."

"This really isn't my kind of job. I'm not a detective or a spy."

"I know that. I could contact the Pinkertons tomorrow, but it would take them two days to get here. I can't wait another two days. I haven't been able to work for a week. I can't concentrate on anything else. I can't get much sleep, either."

If that was true, he was a damned good actor. He'd managed to look and sound very businesslike these past three days since the trouble at the stage station.

"You could ask the sheriff."

He glared at Fargo as if he were stupid. "You're not naive, Fargo. Sheriff Tyndale is a thug. And so are his deputies. Thugs are the only people who can keep a boomtown from coming apart. But you know and I know and so does everybody else that you can't trust them. If I told them this, it would be all over town in an hour. And who knows? They might find out who she's seeing and try to blackmail him."

"You don't have much faith in the people you hired."

"You've seen them, damn it. Do *you* have any faith in them?"

Fargo didn't need to answer that.

Lund continued pacing, went to the window that framed the mountain peaks. "Sometimes it's so damned tempting to just go up into the mountains and never come down. Live out the rest of my life up there." Fargo let him talk at his own pace. "I was never much of a ladies' man. Always too busy with other things. With my first wife, it was no great romance. I loved her and she loved me. We were husband and wife, but in a lot of ways we were brother and sister, too. There was never any question of trust. I would have given my life for her and she would have given her life for me."

He came back from the window and seated himself behind the marble-topped desk. He seemed drained now, weary. "This thing with Alexis—nothing in my life prepared me for it. I walked into a room and saw her and my life was never the same afterward. I had to marry her, possess her. Nothing else mattered. And nothing else matters now, either."

"Maybe you're imagining things." Fargo felt dishonest saying it given what Serena had told him. But he had to pretend that he knew nothing about Alexis or her background.

"I hope I am. God, I hope I am. But I need to be sure." He nodded to Fargo's glass. "How's your brandy?"

"Fine."

"Want more?"

"No, thanks. But I do want to ask you a question."

"Of course."

23

"Do you have some kind of evidence that something's going on with Alexis?"

He leaned back in his cordovan leather chair. "There's a small acreage not too far from here. Whenever I pass by there the elderly lady who sits on the porch waves at me. Every once in a while I stop and talk to her. She always has coffee and the best bread I've ever had. Puts a lot of butter and preserves on it. We have a nice talk about how the Territory was when she and her husband first came out here from Ohio. The last three times I've visited her she's talked about seeing Alexis ride by and head over to where there's a bend in the river."

"Maybe she's just taking a ride."

But his obstinate expression said otherwise. "The same place three times in less than a month? And a part of the country where there's no reason to ride?"

"Have you asked her about it?"

"I've asked her where she went on a particular day. She always has the same answer. She says she just likes to ride along the river."

Fargo set his brandy glass on the desk. "I'm sorry. I just don't want to get involved in this. I'm supposed to start working the northern stage route in two days, anyway."

"Then it'll work out. You've got a couple of days to help me with Alexis."

Serena's words came back to Fargo. She'd want him to help her father. If Fargo could show that Alexis had a lover, Lund would have to confront what his life had become. He almost smiled to himself imagining Serena sliding her slender little hand over his and trying to gently talk him into helping out her father.

"What happens if I turn something up?"

"Then I'll take it from there."

"I don't want to get involved past just telling you what I saw. I'm not going to say anything to her or him—if there's a him."

"I wouldn't expect you to."

"What happens if I find a man with her?"

24

"Then it'll be my problem, and you'll be off working on that stage route. We'll be using that to haul some gold. I want you to help me increase protection for the wagons at the key points."

Fargo stood up. "Well, let me know when you want me to start. Meanwhile, I'll head back to town and get some sleep."

"I want you to start tomorrow morning. She always goes off for a good part of the day on Wednesdays. And you won't need to go back to town for your sleep tonight. I was hoping you'd agree to help me so I had one of the guest cabins prepared for you. It's the one north of the stables. You can come to the house for your breakfast here. You can keep your horse in the stable, of course."

"Your wife won't think it's strange that I'm here?"

"All she'll know is that you're helping me. And you damn well are going to help me."

Fargo wondered if the man might not have slipped over into madness. His body shook now; his eyes bulged slightly; his hands became fists again and again. Fargo sensed that Lund was very near his breaking point.

"I'll walk you to the cabin if you'd like, Fargo."

"I'll be able to find it."

"There'll be a bonus for doing this."

Fargo wondered how a bonus would work. A larger bonus for good news? A smaller bonus for bad?

"I'll be fine." Fargo picked up his hat. "I'll talk to you in the morning."

When Fargo reached the door, Lund said: "I appreciate this, Fargo. Very much." The anger and agitation were gone from his voice. Now there was only sadness.

Fargo fed and watered his Ovaro and bedded him down for the night in the long, clean stable where a dozen other horses were sleeping. He smiled as he watched them in their slumber, many of them snoring, ears, legs, and tails twitching. A horse doc had told him that when a horse was doing this it was probably dreaming. Fargo had always wondered what horses would dream about.

On his way to the guest cabin, he rolled himself a smoke. The night was getting mountain cold but it was good, pure cold. He hoped there were plenty of blankets in the cabin. That was the best kind of sleep. Very cold out, nice and warm in.

He was ten yards from the sizable adobe cabin when he saw a flicker of light through the window. His hand dropped to the Colt he'd strapped on after leaving Lund's mansion. Who the hell would be in his cabin at this hour? Or did he have the wrong cabin? He glanced around to see if there might be another one nearby. But no, this was the only one.

He thought through a couple different approaches for finding out who was inside. He could sneak up to the window and look inside, but he might get his head blown off for the trouble. He could stand in the front and order them to come out with their hands up. But again that might get him shot. Probably the best way— the least bad, as so many things in life came down to—was sneaking up to the door and crashing his way inside. He'd have surprise going for him. And darkness. He'd have a better chance of killing than being killed.

He swung wide toward a shallow copse of pines. From there he watched the side window. There was no flickering light this time. He listened for any sounds, hearing only owls, lonely, distant dogs, and wind.

He pulled his Colt from its holster and proceeded to work his way so that he stood directly in front of the cabin door. There was a flat porch with no steps to climb attached to the front of the place. He'd be able to throw his body against the door with no impediment to slow him down or lessen the impact of his weight smashing against the wood.

He took a deep breath, made sure his grip was tight

on his gun, and then broke into a run aimed straight at the cabin door.

One thing he'd forgotten: that just about any closed door, no matter how flimsy, causes a good deal of pain to the shoulder that splinters it. A tiny shock of surprise raced through his system as the door was popped free of its frame and he rushed inside, Colt ready to deal with any culprit.

"God, Skye, I was going to surprise you."

His eyes hadn't adjusted to the gloom yet. He said, "Serena?"

"Yes." Then she laughed. "The way you came through the door—you really have a flair for drama, don't you?"

"I could've shot you."

"Well, that wouldn't have been very nice now, would it?"

"Where the hell's the lantern?"

"I was trying to light it but the lucifer went out and that was the only one I could find."

The lucifer was what Fargo had seen flickering in the side window.

"Here," he said and went over to the bureau, where he could now make out the shape of the kerosene lamp. He yanked a lucifer from his pocket, scraped it against the bottom of a boot, and brought some light to the room. It was a pleasant place with a double bed, a wardrobe, a small three-shelf case filled with books, and two comfortable overstuffed chairs for sitting. The floor was wood, and heavy quilted rugs covered much of it. A woodstove dominated a far corner.

"The important guests stay in the house, of course," Serena said. "Those are usually Alexis' guests. Dad's guests tend to be some of the men he worked with over the years. Laborers, a lot of them. That's why Alexis had these cabins built. She considers the laborers to be riffraff. Doesn't want them contaminating the hallowed halls of the mansion." She had changed into a white silk blouse and Levi's. "I'm really pathetic, aren't I? How much I hate her, I mean. Half the time I sound like I'm deranged, don't I?"

"I'm too much of a gentleman to answer that."

She poked him in the ribs. "Well, if nothing else, you learned how to two-step tonight."

"Yes, and that'll come in handy someday. Probably save my life." Then he realized that he hadn't asked—or even thought of—the obvious question till now. "How'd you know I would be staying in this cabin tonight?"

She gave him a lazy, winning smile. "I know everything, Mr. Fargo." The smile got wider. "For instance, right now I know what's on your mind because it's the same thing that's on *my* mind."

And with that she began unbuttoning the white blouse. In the lamplight he watched eagerly as the blouse parted to reveal perfectly formed breasts with soft pink nipples that made his crotch tighten and his manhood expand. But the striptease had only begun. She then began to slide off her jeans, the well-shaped hips giving way to the flat stomach and the thatch of dark hair at the top of her legs. She was only a few steps from the bed so she walked backward until she was able to fall down on the mattress. "Why don't you pull my jeans off me, Skye?"

He wasn't about to refuse her request. She lifted her legs and he started sliding the denim off her long, smooth legs. Her musk was intoxicating him.

She didn't waste any time. When the jeans were off, she reached out and took his hand and pulled him down next to her. She slid her fingers between the buttons of his trousers and wriggled them through his underwear until she found him rigid, waiting. Then she pressed him back so that he lay down while she turned her head to bring him a pleasure that was as heady as any wine he'd ever had.

She apparently wanted to take him all the way. But he liked to give pleasure as well as take it. Now it was his turn to press *her* back on the bed. He parted her legs and quickly found the most excitable part of her entire being. She moaned as he began to work carefully to bring her to the first of several peaks they would enjoy during the night.

Following a scream of sheer animal delight, she grabbed his hair with a touch of savagery and brought his face up to hers. Then he was inside her, filling her, driving her on and on to even noisier, blinding treats. His hands cupped her buttocks with enough force to make their groins virtually one as he continued taking them into blinding ecstasy.

Then they lay gasping next to each other. They didn't talk at first. There was nothing to say. She waited several minutes before saying: "I don't suppose you'd like to go again, would you?"

He laughed. "I thought you'd never ask."

4

She was a good horsewoman.

But she wasn't much fun to follow.

Alexis Lund had left the mansion at seven o'clock. It was now nearing nine, and so far she had stopped at a small café and sat in a chair outside a blacksmith's shop where inside one of her horse's shoes was being replaced.

Fargo had stayed at a discreet distance, walking his Ovaro off road whenever possible. Alexis was in no hurry and only twice did she make her pinto do much more than simply walk.

She wore a tan silk blouse and brown butternuts. Her hair was pulled back into a chignon. Not a single man she passed failed to stop and look at her. The sunlight limned her in gold, goddesslike.

Fargo knew it was too early to make any judgment about her. There was always the possibility that Serena was wrong about her. That something about Lund had changed her, made her the faithful woman she might have longed to become. Living was a strange business and people, sometimes the worst of them, surprised you.

After she was finished at the blacksmith's, Alexis turned her pinto toward the river. This time the horse moved at a trot and finally into a run.

The speed of the horse made him decide that Serena's suspicions were probably correct. Alexis was going somewhere that really meant something to her.

Either she was late for an appointment or she was headed toward a meeting that made her blood race.

They were soon in the foothills. There were animals in addition to the usual cows and horses. In the course of the ride Fargo saw moose and elk; a bear lay on a ledge of rock watching the road in the distance. There was a comic aspect to this; he could have been an old gent. All he needed was a corncob pipe.

Alexis turned abruptly away from the trail and headed behind a chain of tall, plump boulders that lay on a steep incline. She disappeared.

For the first time today Fargo knew he had to be careful. This was where he could be caught following her. He had no idea what lay behind the boulders. He even thought that she might be on to him and had ducked in here as part of a trap. She was a smart woman.

Taking his Ovaro behind the boulders would be too dangerous. He led the stallion over to a grassy area and ground-tied him. Then, drawing his Colt, he made his way toward the boulders. When he reached the bottom rock, he took off his hat and dropped it to the ground. He needed to peek around the boulder, and the hat would give him away for sure.

He steadied himself and leaned forward for a quick look. Alexis Lund stood on a low hill in the arms of a man. Their kiss was passionate. The man ran his hands up and down her body. And she clung to him almost savagely.

Behind them he could see a cabin, a well-tended structure with smoke curling out of the chimney and chickens walking around frantically.

He needed only one more detail. The identity of the man. He probably wouldn't know his name but he could at least get a useful description of him. Right now all he could see was that the man had long dark hair. His hands looked swarthy against the tan of her blouse.

But it still wasn't good enough for Fargo. He needed a closer observation of the man. Two big problems. How would he get up the slope here without being seen? And could he even make it up there before the two inevitably went inside the shack? He could wait them out but what if the man stayed behind in the shack afterward and she came down the slope? There'd be no place for him to hide.

The man combed his fingers into her hair and their embrace became even more desperate, urgent. Then they parted and she laughed with such great sexual joy she sounded half insane. She put her hand in his and they angled themselves toward the cabin.

She started to pull him up the grassy incline. The man took his first real step. He limped on his right leg. Perceptibly. Fargo wondered if the man had simply gotten a charley horse. But as the man continued to walk, Fargo saw the shoe on his right leg was built up, the way shoes were for people who'd been born with one leg shorter than the other.

Fargo had the mark of identification he needed.

"What the hell'd you do to this man?" old Doc Standish said to Sheriff Harve Tyndale.

"Is he dead?"

"Damned near, thanks to you."

They were in one of the eight cells situated in back of the front office of the sheriff's department. A man lay on his back on one of the thin cots. The man and the cot alike showed bright splatters of blood. The man was around thirty, and chunky. His breathing came in painful gasps—almost asthmatic sounding—and his head had so many knots, bumps, and contusions that the small, bald Doc Standish hadn't been able to count them all.

"I guess he must've fallen down."

Harve Tyndale was six-three, weighed two-twenty, and had been a bare-knuckle fighter for a few years in and around Denver and Cheyenne. He took an unseemly—hell, *unholy*—delight in beating prisoners to the point where four or five a year died "under mysterious circumstances," as the judge always insisted when ruling that a given inquest was over and no further inquiry was needed.

Doc Standish had worked boomtowns before. Law enforcement in raw, rich towns was always merciless. And actually seeing a man pounded into a stupor, even a coma, by the likes of Tyndale and his deputies had never bothered Standish much until his third son, Nick, had left home and moved to Denver, where he was constantly in and out of trouble thanks to a taste for cheap whiskey and cheaper women. A year ago he had decided to pay his twenty-year-old son a surprise visit. He'd found him in the Denver municipal jail. Nick had come along by accident late in the lives of Myrtle and Doc Standish. Myrtle had developed what was to Doc an unwholesome relationship with the boy. When he so much as bruised a knee she became hysterical. She was overprotective to a degree that their friends found amusing and he found disgusting. Imagine what she'd think seeing her boy in a dank, shadowy cell with his head split open, his right eye closed, and three of his front teeth missing. For the first time Standish realized that he'd been a participant in this kind of inexcusable violence for many years. He'd paid the boy's bail, taken him to a hotel room, and stayed in Denver until the boy could stand up without being dizzy, hold down food, and not have a headache that felt as if it was cleaving his skull in half.

He'd returned to Reliance unable to patch up the near dead without at least complaining to Tyndale and his men about their unnecessary treatment of prisoners.

"This man needs to be brought to my office right away. He'll have to stay in one of the beds there for at least two days."

"I can't spare the man to guard him."

Standish, who had a neat white beard and a trim sixty-six-year-old body, said, "Then you'll have a corpse in the cell by sundown."

"I've had corpses in my cells before, Doc."

Standish, who was a mere five-seven, turned on Tyndale with the ferocity of an angry dog. He even poked him in the chest. "I want this man brought to my office right now. Do you understand me, Tyndale?"

He could see that Tyndale was prepared to make a joke of the moment—a silly-ass little medical man trying to intimidate a man like Tyndale—but then he checked himself. Doc had a lot of friends in Reliance. A lot more friends than Tyndale did. And the election was coming up. Lund fielded both slates—both opponents were his men, bought and paid for—but he gave the voters a choice of which bought-and-paid-for man most appealed to them. And it was well known that Lund wanted to get rid of Tyndale. He'd served his purpose. He'd tamed the town, a violent man being necessary for the task. The town still had its share of troubles but these days Tyndale still reacted as he had when he'd first come here, and murder was commonplace. Tyndale was well aware that Lund wanted him gone.

"You got a bug up your ass today or somethin', Doc?"

"Yes, I do, Tyndale. I get tired of seeing men like these. What he'd do, get drunk and say something to one of your deputies? Or one of your deputies was bored so he decided to push him into a fight? Or somebody had a grudge against this man so he talked your deputy into beating him?"

Tyndale saw there was no use arguing. "I'll have him brought over, Doc."

Standish didn't move. He seemed to be studying Tyndale's face, as if there were a secret there that he wanted to know. "I'll be honest with you, Tyndale. I'll be glad when you're gone."

Tyndale grabbed his arm. "Don't talk to me that way, damn you."

"Take your hand off me."

Tyndale withdrew his hand. Forced himself to calm down. "I'll try and watch myself in the future, Doc. How's that?"

"That go for your deputies, too?"

"I'll see that it does."

After the doc left, Tyndale went over to his desk, sat down, pulled out the pint bottle, and had himself a good hard belt. The hell of it was he liked this town. He had everything arranged. He had certain privileges at the saloons, the whorehouses, the outlaw hideouts in the hills, even at church. On Sundays he was an usher at church. He could see his old man smirking about that. His old man never had any time for people who put on airs, and he'd considered church ushers among the worst of them. Whenever the old lady would drag him to Mass the old man would bitch for days afterward about the ushers, saying they were sissies and ass-kissers and sickening spectacles of manhood.

Yeah, the old man would laugh his ass off if he was still alive and knew that his boy was an usher.

Tyndale had another drink.

For a moment there he'd forgotten his election troubles. But now they were back. It was too late to win voters over with promises. Farnham, his opponent, was already promising everything under the sun. Plus Tyndale had the suspicion that the gentry was behind Farnham. He was young and good-looking, and he'd gone through eighth grade, a point he alluded to in his speeches. He characterized Tyndale as a hairy barbarian who had done a good job of cleaning out riffraff because he was riffraff himself and thus knew how to handle them. But now that Reliance was becoming a real town with a real town council and a real school and a real future . . . Well, there wasn't any room in a town like that for riffraff, was there?

What he needed, Tyndale knew, was to do something that would impress the voters so much that they would see him for the capable lawman he was—so capable in fact that they would forget or at least overlook his overly enthusiastic jailhouse procedures. They would compare Tyndale to Farnham at that moment and see that there was really no contest here. Experience and maturity versus pretty words and a young face. And no experience. And no maturity.

What was it he could do? Nothing came to mind.

But something had better damned soon come to mind. The election might be two months away but if the doc was any indication, a whole lot of voters had already made up their minds.

All the way back to the mansion Fargo felt a growing resentment for having been dragged into Lund's personal affairs. This wasn't Fargo's kind of work. Now he'd have to face a man and tell him that his wife was being unfaithful. And then he'd have to see the impact of his words on the man's daughter. Serena had not only been a most nubile partner in bed, but he also liked her. She wasn't anything like most of the young, wealthy girls he'd met over the years. She had a sense of humor about herself and she loved her father in a simple, unfettered way, not just because he was a powerful man.

The mansion gleamed as the sun climbed to noon. Armed guards patrolled the perimeter of the grounds in military fashion. At the front entrance—the only entrance—two armed guards noted the coming and going of every human, vehicle, and horse that passed beneath the tall stone arch.

Fargo nodded to the guards as he rode his Ovaro up the winding road toward the massive house, its turrets and spires like something out of an adventure book. He dismounted, walked his stallion over to the stable, and rewarded him for a good day's work. He could have done all this later. But right now he would do anything to avoid going into the mansion and telling Lund what he'd seen.

He was just leaving the stable when Serena rode up. Her outfit today was a yellow sweater with a green silk scarf, tight jeans, and leather boots that came up to her knees. Her mount was sleek and the color of chestnuts. She dropped from the saddle and walked her horse over to the stable door.

"I take it you'll be gracing us with your presence at dinner tonight, Skye."

"Maybe."

A man came from inside the stable and took her horse. She joined Fargo on his way to the house, shedding her leather gloves as they walked.

"Any particular reason you're so quiet, Skye?"

"Just sort of tired, I guess."

For a time they let the birds and the wind make the sounds and then Serena burst out: "You found out something, didn't you?"

"Huh-uh."

She stopped him and took his arm. "You followed her and she met somebody, didn't she?" She was childishly excited.

"I need to talk to your father before I say anything. He's the one who hired me."

They neared the house but she steered away to the right, toward the large white gazebo that lay like a shrine to summer in the center of an open space.

"You're kidnapping me," he laughed.

"You're damned right I am."

She dragged him up the three steps and inside the white gazebo. In the summer this would be festooned with flowers and colorful lanterns. It was less romantic this afternoon, what with one of the big collies who roamed the grounds having had a formidable bowel movement only a few feet away from the gazebo itself.

"Who was she with?"

"You know a man with a built-up shoe?"

"Oh, God, Skye. That's Carstairs. The painter. He's from New York. He came out here to do a series of paintings for a museum back there."

"Well, she rode up into the hills and met him."

"Yes, he has a cabin up there."

He described what he'd seen.

At first she'd sounded pleased about what he'd been able to discover, but as he talked he watched her pleasure change to dread. She had reached the same realization that he had. Maybe the titillation of it all was amusing but the amusement stopped when she realized what this would do to her father when Fargo gave him his report. Alexis was his life. He might have suspected her of being unfaithful, but suspecting was far different from knowing.

"Poor Dad."

"Yeah."

"I wonder what he'll do."

"I don't intend to stick around and find out."

"You're leaving?"

"Soon as I talk to your father, I'm mounting up and riding away."

"But why?"

"Because this isn't my kind of work. I have to go in there and tell him that his wife is being untrue to him. What the hell kind of job is that?"

"There you are, Serena."

The voice came clear and strong in the late afternoon. The master of the house. Lund came striding across the grounds in a brown leather jacket and white shirt and brown trousers. His white Stetson caught the fading streams of sunlight.

"Maria's looking for you in the kitchen. She's making that pot roast we like so much. But she said she needs you to help her."

"I showed her how to season it a little better."

"Well, then you'd better get in there."

Fargo could feel the other man's tension. The story about the cook needing Serena might possibly be a lie. But when Lund saw Fargo he wanted to talk to him immediately and alone. A fib was permissible.

Serena glanced from her father to Skye. Dread filled her lovely eyes. She could almost feel the pain that would be visited upon her father. She said, "I'll be in the house."

"Thank you," Lund said.

They watched her leave, watched her walk up to the house, then watched the doorway she'd entered. Fargo didn't want to talk and Lund didn't want to listen. But neither man had a choice.

"I'm pretty good at reading faces, Fargo."

"Oh?"

"And I can tell you've got some bad news for me."

Fargo wanted to get on his horse and ride away without having to tell the man that his wife was indeed seeing somebody else on the side.

"You want to sit in the gazebo?"

"Just get to it, Fargo." Then: "Who is it?"

Fargo sighed. "I didn't want this job."

"Damn it, Fargo. You obviously saw her with somebody today. I want to know his name."

"A man with a short leg. Carstairs is his name, I guess."

"Carstairs? A cripple?"

For a powerful man like Lund this had to be particularly devastating news. Not only was his wife's lover not wealthy but he was not a whole man, either. And what an unmanly calling—painting on canvas every day.

"Carstairs? You're sure?"

Fargo described the day following her and how it had culminated at the cabin. When he finished, he realized that his words hadn't stoked Lund's anger. They seemed to have made him weary instead. He looked his true age now, a sad older man.

Barely whispering, he said, "I trusted her. I trusted her completely."

"I'm sorry."

"I've always sensed that Serena didn't trust her but I thought she might be jealous. She's used to having all my attention, especially since her mother died. But obviously Serena was right."

Fargo almost said that maybe there was some other explanation but he caught himself in time. What a stupid thing to say. What the hell other explanation could there be?

Lund focused on him. "You want to get as far away from this thing as you can, don't you?"

"This isn't in my line of work. As I mentioned."

Lund laughed bitterly. "I wish I could get away from it, too. Just get on a horse and ride so far away nobody would ever find me again."

Fargo had a lot of misgivings about the man, particularly in the way he treated his miners and in the way he hired gunslicks for lawmen, but at the moment he felt sorry for him. Lund was confounded by the news. As Fargo probably would have been, too.

"I'll have to talk to her, won't I?" The longer he talked, the more helpless he sounded. This powerful man, helpless. "I'll have to tell her that I had her followed and then I'll have to tell her what I found out. And she'll lie to me, won't she, Fargo?"

"Probably."

Lund took a deep breath, let it out. "I need to go back to my study. Have a little brandy. Think this thing through. The best way to approach her, I mean."

Lund was still at the point where he couldn't quite face what he'd learned. When that moment came, the helplessness would become bitterness. Or maybe even something worse.

"I'd like to start tomorrow on that other work you mentioned," Fargo said.

Lund seemed confused. "What other work?"

"The stage routes. Seeing how to protect them. The strategic points, the way I did with the other one."

"Oh, yes. Of course." But Lund still didn't sound as if he was sure of what was going on here. He turned away in fact, his eyes narrowing on the mansion. His wife wasn't home yet but probably would be soon. He'd mentioned his study and some brandy. He damned sure needed something right now. "I was only unfaithful to her once. But I have a feeling that she's made a habit out of cheating on me."

He didn't say good-bye. He didn't even nod. He just walked away. He usually had a long and assertive stride. Not now. Shoulders slumped, footsteps unsteady, he made slow, uncertain progress as he returned to his house.

Fargo knew that Serena would soon reappear. But he didn't want to talk about the matter anymore. He wanted to be done with it all.

Soon Fargo was on his way back to town.

5

She was naked, a young, ripe, appealing woman sitting on the edge of the canopy bed in the master bedroom, and Brett Norton felt no desire for her whatsoever. The large pink nipples; the flat stomach angling down to the dark area between her legs; the attractive if not pretty face; and Brett Norton . . . the blond stallion (or so he thought himself) who could mount and ride a woman no matter how drunk he was . . . Brett Norton felt no desire whatsoever.

Louise was the daughter of the maid who tended to all of bachelor Norton's needs. He'd sent her to the general store twenty minutes ago so he could be alone with nineteen-year-old Louise. They'd been together six or seven times in the past month. She was excited to be with someone so rich and courtly. She'd confessed that she was tired of the young miners and farm boys who always called on her. Norton had no feelings for her except lust. And right now he felt not even that.

Her blue eyes looked troubled. "Don't you like me anymore?" she whined, noting that he had yet to take his clothes off. The room was decorated with military ornaments from the time of King Arthur. A shield, a battle ax, mace, a broadsword, and other deadly pieces of warfare. Replicas, of course, but damned good ones shipped over from England. He amused himself with the notion that in the master bedroom he made war on the female species. And he triumphed every time.

Except this afternoon.

He willed his manhood to stiffen but got no response. He saw how she parted her legs slightly. She was a tasty sweet thing, no doubt about it.

"I can help you," she said. "One of the boys who used to call on me, I had to help *him* sometimes."

"Don't be ridiculous," he snapped. "I don't need any of your so-called help. I just remembered something I have to do. That's all."

He could see that she didn't believe him. Was that a tiny smile fretting the right corner of her full lips? Little bitch. Laughing at him, was she? No, Louise wouldn't laugh at him. She was too intimidated by him.

"Get up and get dressed."

"But—I thought you liked being with me."

And then she did the worst damned thing of all.

She started crying. Sitting there completely naked, crying, her breasts trembling with her sorrow. She put her hands over her face like a small girl.

"It's not that, Louise. It's just what I told you. I forgot that I had something to do. Now please get up and put your clothes on and let me work."

She did as she was told. He appreciated the young, firm curves of her body as she tugged on her undergarments and then the brown gingham dress that only seemed to enhance her body rather than hide it. The crying ended but she was still sniffling.

After she finished with her poor, cheap shoes she came over to him and said, "Will you want me to come back here again?"

"Of course. Of course I will. Now go downstairs and wait for your mother."

She stood on tiptoe and kissed him tenderly on the mouth. "I think about you all the time."

After she was gone, he thought: *Bitch.*

But he didn't have Louise in mind. Oh, no, Louise was too feckless to be a bitch. To be a real bitch a woman had to be a manipulator, a conniver, a liar, a whore.

There was only one woman like that in Norton's life, the woman he feared he was doomed to be in love with the rest of his life: Alexis Lund.

It always struck him as bitterly funny that he'd spent most of his thirty-eight years taking the women he wanted and then running quickly away from them without a single regret. When they cried to him that he had misled and betrayed them, he pretended to be shocked. *I didn't mean to make you think this was serious; I'm sorry.* It helped that many of his conquests had been married—a spurned married woman could protest only so much without revealing her affair to her husband.

And, at first, Alexis, beautiful as she was, looked to be another easy conquest. Poor Alexis. Lund was a dull old man. No wonder she fell so easily into Norton's arms. He had no idea then that he would fall in love with her. That he would come to a time when he couldn't eat, sleep, think coherently because of her. Or would destroy his office one day in a fit of rage so terrifying that his secretary ran to get the minister, seriously thinking that Norton had become possessed by the devil.

That was the day he discovered he wasn't her only lover.

He went over to the canopy bed and sank down on the edge of it. There had to be some way to make her change her ways. Had to·be some way to make her put it back the way it had been. Had to be some way to make her spend hours with him in this very bed when the maid and other servants were gone.

Had to be; had to be.

She had waited for this moment for more than four years, but now that it was here it terrified her because she had never heard her father this angry.

She heard something smashing—thrown, she imagined—against the wall in the study, then a scream. Something else smashed against the wall. Her father shouted, thundered at Alexis. As much as she usually liked to spy on the people in her father's study, tonight she stayed in her bedroom with the door closed. But it didn't matter. The roar of the argument filled the entire mansion. She knew that the four servants would be cowering in the kitchen, not knowing what to do. And by now, given her father's shouting, they obviously knew what had prompted this rage.

Alexis had been unfaithful.

Now there was sobbing. This was the only part Serena wished she could see: Alexis humbled. Even if the tears were faked, Alexis would not dare be dismissive or haughty with Serena's father now. Even if she planned to flee into the arms of Carstairs, she would have to endure the verbal punishment that Lund was inflicting on her. And by the sound of things, would continue to inflict on her for some time.

Serena wished she were taking more pleasure in this. But in wanting to prevent pain for her father—wishing that Alexis would be exposed—she realized now that his pain bordered on madness. For the first time in her life she was afraid of what her father might do.

Another crash sounded as something heavy was turned over. Alexis screamed. Her father's voice was so loud Serena was surprised the walls didn't shake.

On impulse she started to the door. She intended to burst in to the study and calm her father down, not for Alexis' sake but for her father's. She would tell Alexis to pack up and get out. And then when she was alone with her father she would assure him that as bad as he felt now, in time he would see that this was for the best, that Alexis had been a schemer all along. He was still a strapping, powerful man and he would find a good woman to be his wife. And—yes—Serena would help him. How would that be? The idea amused her. Father and daughter on a wife hunt for the father. She would go right downstairs now and tell him.

She got as far as putting her hand on the doorknob, then stopped. She was being ridiculous. If she did any of the things she'd just thought of, her father would get even angrier.

She walked back to the window seat where she'd often sat as a child, contemplating the night sky and wondering if cows really did jump over the moon as in one of the stories her mother had always read her.

Oh, Lord, it would be so good to be that child again, innocent of human ways, her mother alive and her father so happy.

It would be so very, very good.

And then she heard the words she had yearned to hear ever since Alexis had first entered the house: "All right, then, Andrew! I'm leaving! I'll be staying at the Reliance Hotel until further notice!"

A door slammed, Alexis making as much noise as possible.

Alexis was leaving!

6

Today might just be the day, Fargo thought as he watched the waitress named Myrna set down a plate filled with steak, sliced potatoes, and corn in front of him. She'd already brought him three cups of coffee while he waited for his food and in the course of it had told him that she finished work as soon as the lunch hour was over.

Miners, cowboys, sharpers of various kinds, and couples from town filled the place that was draped in cigarette and cigar smoke.

Myrna was a lithe redhead with amused green eyes and a slim but well-developed body. There was an air of fun about her, the way she teased, the soft sarcasm, the occasional coy hint that she was available. Today she was making the hint more explicit.

The café was busy and a few customers were getting impatient with the amount of time she spent with the handsome drifter. But if she cared about their irritation, she didn't let on. "I suppose an old duffer like you needs an afternoon nap, though."

"I bet you could use a nap, too."

He liked her clean, sharp laugh.

"Think you could stay awake long enough to have a visitor?"

"I'd probably have to drink a lot more coffee."

"Well, we've got plenty of that."

"Then maybe I'll have one more cup with my food and head back to my room at the Excelsior."

"And from what I hear that would be room 214."

He smiled up at her. "You wouldn't be one of those gypsy women who can read minds, would you?"

"No, but I would have a cousin who works there behind the front desk sometimes."

"That's even better than a gypsy woman."

She finally relented and went back to her other customers. They were all easily mollified by her competence—now that she *wanted* to be competent—and that great, clever smile of hers.

Fifteen minutes later Fargo walked back to his hotel amidst all the clamor of a boomtown: a stray shot from a six-shooter, probably harmless; a fistfight in an alleyway; a pair of soiled doves trying to convince two elderly drunks that they could make them young again; a respectable middle-aged woman sobbing; a young man puking; and over all, the beat and slam and grind of the mines themselves. He'd be glad to be done with it and back to the relative peace of the stage routes. He'd rather face outlaws than a sham of a town like this one.

In his room he washed up, rolled himself a smoke, took a reasonable-size snort from a pint of rye he'd bought earlier, and then parked himself on his bed. He'd left the door unlocked.

She was there even sooner than he'd thought she would be.

"Alms for the poor," she said as she peeked inside.

She wore a dark cape over her work dress. Her red hair had been tousled by the wind. The wind had also colored her cheeks and made her look even younger and more adventurous.

"I hope you realize that I'm a virgin, Mr. Fargo."

"Well, what a coincidence."

"You, too?" She was already disposing of the cape and starting to work on her dress.

"Yes, I wanted to wait until I was sure I was old enough to start committing sins of the flesh."

"I'm told they can be a lot of fun, those sins." She was now down to her undergarments and walking toward him as she dropped them on the floor.

She had pert young breasts with long nipples the color of salmon. Her hips curved perfectly, trailing into long thighs topped by a crimson bush. She also had a very sexual way of walking, one that instantly inspired a stiffening of Fargo's attention.

"Any room for me on this bed?" she said, playfully taking his cigarette from him. She stabbed it out in the tin ashtray on the chair and then pushed him over so she could lie down.

He reached for her and brought her face down to his. Their mouths opened and he felt the sweet warmth of her breath and the urgent, flicking passion of her tongue. His hands found her full, eager breasts, the pink areolas bright in the slanting sunlight. He lapped them until the nipples became firm nubs that rubbed his eyes as she drew him close to her.

The transformation was almost magical. They moved with such need that they were scarcely aware of her slipping his pants off, of her sliding her legs over his shoulders, of him lancing deep into the hot juices of her sex. The position allowed him to strike deep as she clamped her hands to his buttocks for maximum connection.

She whispered: "Make it last, Fargo. I need this."

His strokes became longer, more deliberate, as he took his time bringing her to the moment when her eyes glistened with sensual joy and her body writhed wildly. She eased him off and then rolled over, presenting herself so that he could take her from behind. This was a woman who knew what she wanted and Fargo appreciated that. She was a skilled partner.

His hands entangled in her brilliant red hair, he brought them to mutual climax only after her whispers signaled that she was ready for it. Then they fell side by side, Fargo close enough to his makings so that after a time he could roll a cigarette.

"I don't suppose you'd give me a couple of puffs of that," she said.

"Well," he grinned, "I suppose that could be arranged."

*   *   *

Fargo wasn't sure if the knocking was in his dream or in reality. He'd been sleeping comfortably after the redhead had gone so he was lazy responding to the banging on the door. It was getting on to six o'clock, full dark now.

He grabbed his Colt from the holster hanging from the brass head of the bed. The knock was insistent, desperate.

He eased himself from the bed and walked across the floor on tiptoe. He stood to the side of the door and said, "Who is it?"

"It's Serena, Skye. Let me in. Hurry. Please." He didn't have to see her to know that she was crying.

He opened the door and she fell into his arms. The weeping she'd had under control now burst forth in a series of body-jolting sobs. He helped her to the bed and hurried to close the door and turn up the lamp. He grabbed his pint of rye and put it to her lips. Her face smelled of cold and tears.

After he got two large gulps down her, she began forcing herself to calm down. She took deep breaths and wiped away tears that made her eyes shimmer in the lamplight.

What the hell had happened, Fargo wondered, to bring her here?

He didn't have to wait long for the answer.

"It's Alexis, Skye," she said in a single gasp. "Somebody murdered her and I'm afraid my father did it."

7

Sheriff Harve Tyndale stared at the dead woman in the blue silk robe. He was pretty sure she was naked underneath. He'd always tried to imagine Alexis Lund naked, and now—way too late—he was going to get his chance.

This was taking place in room 204 of the Reliance Hotel, the most expensive, exclusive, elite hotel in the Territory. The mattresses were thick, the furnishings British, and the service impeccable. The local joke was that this was where the gentrified men of Reliance brought their women for trysts with their golden rods.

Sheriff Tyndale knew that this room represented the way he was going to get back at Andrew Lund for dumping him and supporting a new candidate for sheriff. Who had a better reason to kill Alexis Lund than her angry husband? Tyndale knew all about her lovers, but he was going to make sure that it was Lund he arrested for her murder.

The bone-handled knife that had ripped into a narrow spot just above her right breast looked especially ugly from where he stood.

But ugly as it was, this was a happy moment for the lawman. He was soon going to pay Lund back for turning against him.

She'd made herself at home. Perfumes were lined up like toy soldiers on the dressing table and the closet held four different dresses. He'd checked the bureaus and found two drawers containing her undergarments.

He needed to find out when she'd checked in. He needed to learn everything he could about what had brought her here.

He heard loud talk coming from the stairs. At first there were two, maybe three voices talking over each other—arguing. Then it sounded as if one man had broken from the others and was pounding up the rest of the steps. Then he heard a female voice, young.

There was a heavy knock on the door. Who the hell was it? Why hadn't his deputies stopped them?

He pushed himself up from the bed and walked to the door. Fargo and Serena stood there, gawkers crowded around them.

Tyndale put out a big hand. Fargo and Serena walked under it. Tyndale slammed the door behind them. He knew he had to be careful. He had to play it like he was a responsible lawman trying to find out who the killer was. Right now he couldn't afford to make any accusations about Lund.

"Oh, Lord. Lord," Serena said. Tyndale noted that she didn't cry when she said this. Nor did her small, lovely face reflect shock or horror. She was simply noting the dead woman.

"You wouldn't happen to know where your father is, would you?" Tyndale said.

She turned on him. "What's that supposed to mean?"

"It was a question, miss. Nothing more. This is his wife. She's been killed. Seems reasonable to me that somebody should tell him."

Tyndale could see Fargo watching him carefully. Right now Fargo would be wondering if the lawman had donned a clever mask. Where was all the corn-pone bullying? The bragging? The arrogance? This couldn't be Tyndale, could it?

Serena said, "I suppose he's at home."

"Any idea what your stepmother was doing here?"

Serena hesitated, her eyes flicking to Fargo's. Obviously she wanted to speak carefully. "They—they had an argument."

"I see. When was this?"

"Early this afternoon."

"Any idea what they argued about?"

"No." But she'd said it too quickly.

"And she left then?"

She slid her hand in Fargo's. "Do I have to talk to him?"

Fargo shrugged. "He's doing his job." He sounded surprised.

"My father was home. He didn't have anything to do with this, if that's what you're thinking, Tyndale."

"You're the one who brought it up, miss. I just asked about your stepmother. Were you there when she left?"

"Yes."

"Looks like she packed some clothes and things."

"Yes. She told my father she was leaving."

"Did your father try to stop her?"

"No."

"They had an argument and she just walked out?"

"Yes."

"Sort of cooling things off, were they?"

"If you want to put it that way." Serena was speaking to Tyndale but once again her eyes were fixed on Alexis. The cheeks were paler now, the eyes glassier. Death was taking her completely and finally.

"How'd you find out about this, Miss Lund?"

"I was in town to meet Mr. Fargo. On my way to the café I saw people standing in the doorway of the hotel. Looking like something was wrong. I thought I heard somebody call my name."

It was a lie and the shakiness of her voice betrayed it. But Tyndale went on: "So you came up to the room?"

"No. I—I went into the lobby. I heard what had happened. Then I ran to meet Skye—Mr. Fargo. I didn't want to come up here alone."

"Can't say I blame you for that."

"That's very understanding of you, Tyndale."

He smiled. "I'm sorry if I offended you, miss. Like Fargo here said, I'm just trying to do my job."

"I'd like to go."

"I can't blame you there, either."

She took Fargo's hand. "I'd like to get a drink of whiskey downstairs."

He nodded to Tyndale.

Serena half dragged Fargo to the door. The number of gawkers had doubled. They had to push their way through the wall of flesh.

8

Melissa Holmes was reading her copy of *Peterson's Magazine*—her favorite among magazines for ladies—when she heard her husband, James, come in the back door of their three-story brick home. The servants were already in their quarters in their cabin and she'd been enjoying the warmth of the fire, the creak of the rocking chair (the same chair her mother used to rock her in back when they'd lived in Maine), and the tart taste of the warm apple cider. James always joked that she was an old woman before her time. "You're forty-one but sometimes you act like you're ninety." But she didn't care. She wasn't like the wives of other prominent men, in some sort of competition to see who the fanciest, smartest, and most appealing was.

But as always when she got smug about herself, she realized that James would never have become so infatuated with Alexis Lund if he'd had a sparkling wife to come home to.

She put down her magazine and listened as James made his way through the kitchen and into the small room off the hallway where he liked to wash up before coming into the living room. But usually he called out hello. And usually he made a bit more noise than he did tonight.

When he did appear, coming through the archway, he looked strangely tense. Not even a forced smile could conceal his mood, or the fact that he'd been drinking.

James Holmes, an icon of probity, a master of self-control, a symbol of all that was moderate, moral, and desirable in life, had actually overimbibed. In eighteen years of marriage—childless years, alas—she could never remember seeing him overimbibe.

"Quit looking at me that way."

"I'm just surprised is all, James."

"Surprised that your husband is a little drunk?"

She smiled. "You're more than a little drunk, honey. Did you and some of the tellers have one of those poker games?" A few times a year, to show his bank employees that he appreciated their labors, he'd stay after work and play poker for a few hours. He always came home with beer on his breath, but never drunk.

He carefully crossed the room and set himself with great precision on the couch that had been imported from New York. "Would you mind not squeaking?" he said. His words were slurred.

"The chair squeaking, you mean?"

"The chair squeaking. Of course. I didn't mean *you* squeaking, did I?"

At any other time they both would have had a laugh over the idiocy of this.

"It's a restful sound. You said so yourself."

"Well, I'm not saying it tonight. Tonight it's an irritating sound."

She stopped rocking and set the magazine on her lap. She was suddenly afraid. She wasn't sure why. All she knew was that something was wrong here. This man on the couch was an imposter, rude and angry. Where was her husband, the real James? Something terrible must have happened.

"Did the poker game go well?"

He sat like a penitent little boy, his stubby hands folded together on his lap, his eyes downcast. He spoke softly now. "There wasn't any game."

"Did you stop off at your club?"

"No."

He still didn't look up at her.

55

Alexis, she knew. For the past two years she'd known of his obsession with the woman. She'd found a foolish letter he'd written Alexis, never mailed. She never mentioned it. They'd go for weeks without making love. He'd be distracted. Moody. But never like this. She wondered now if her silent plan to simply wait until his obsession ended had been a good idea after all.

Even more, she wondered what had happened to put him in a mood like this tonight.

"Would you like some supper?"

"No." Then, more like James instead of the imposter: "No, thanks."

"Food would probably make you feel better." She wished he'd raise those gray eyes of his to hers. She'd always loved the tender way he'd looked at her in the early years of their marriage.

She stood up. Maybe if she fixed him some food, the smells of it would entice him to eat. The food and some coffee would help bring him around. She was sure of it.

"You just sit here and relax. I'll set a place for you at the table."

If he heard, he didn't let on.

She was halfway to the kitchen when she heard the most extraordinary sound she'd ever heard James make. Sitting all alone in their comfortable living room before a warming fire and with the prospect of a good meal before him, James Albert Holmes let out something very much like a sob.

It was close to midnight before Lund appeared in his town office where Serena and Fargo waited for him. He wore a duster, a dark Stetson, and a pair of red-rimmed eyes. He smelled of the cold night and of whiskey.

Serena had told the sheriff that they'd wait here for her father to be summoned from the mansion and brought to town.

Lund took his hat and duster off and walked

straight to a mahogany bookcase in the corner of the office. He took down a fat volume that appeared to be a law book, opened it, and withdrew a pint of whiskey from inside. In other circumstances this would have been funny, the boss hiding the liquor. But not now, not tonight.

Serena had started to say something but stopped herself. She sat perched nervously on the edge of a chair. Her eyes followed her father from the bookcase to where he finally seated himself behind his desk. She looked terrified. Fargo wondered if this was because she was upset in general or because she suspected that her father had snuck into town and killed his wife.

Lund poured whiskey into a coffee cup.

"According to Tyndale I killed Alexis."

"Oh, Dad, he can't really believe that."

"He does. Obviously. And he was kind enough to tell me about all the men he suspects she was sleeping with."

She went to him, stood over him, kissed him on top of his head, and then kept her face next to his momentarily. He patted her hand. She went back and sat down in the chair next to Fargo.

"He hates me because he knows I want him gone," Lund said. "That's why I put up a better man in this election. Tyndale got too brutal. Everybody was complaining about him."

"You let him run," Fargo said. "You could have reined him in."

Serena and her father turned on Fargo instantly. "You don't have any right to speak to my father that way."

"I was occupied with running my businesses. I wasn't aware of everything he was doing." Then, sadly: "Just as I didn't know everything my wife was doing." His gaze was somber. "I guess you were right, honey. I never should have trusted her."

"You should fire him right now, Dad."

"No," Fargo said. "If you're innocent, that's the worst thing you could do. Tyndale's dropped his

57

bullyboy mask. He's a lot smarter than most people give him credit for. If you fire him, he'll tell everybody that he knew you were guilty and that's why he had to be pushed out."

Lund nodded. "When we interviewed him several years back, he came across as a very sharp operator. But as soon as he was put on the badge, out came the hard-assed side of him. We didn't care. He made a lot of headway cleaning up this town. You might think it's still wild, Fargo, but you should have seen it back then."

"Nobody will believe you killed Alexis, Dad. You loved her too much."

Lund grimaced. "Honey, nobody has more enemies than a rich man. Just about everybody in town will think I'm guilty, especially if Tyndale starts saying so to everybody who owns a pair of ears."

"Then what can we do?"

Lund raised his eyes to meet Fargo's. "You told me that you worked with the Pinkertons a few times."

Fargo shook his head. "It's not even worth talking about. I wouldn't be any help to you at all."

The demons came then. Lund raised a powerful fist over his head and brought it smashing down against the top of his desk. "How could she have lied to me that way? I loved her so damned much!" he shouted.

Fargo had been wondering about Lund's strange emotionless appearance in the office. Now he realized that the man had simply been restraining his true feelings.

Serena started to leave her chair, go to him once again, but Fargo stopped her.

"Did you sneak into town and see her?" Fargo said to the man who sat there staring down at his desk and shaking his head.

"Of course he didn't, Skye. Don't even think such a thing."

Lund nodded to his daughter. "She's right, Skye. I didn't go to town."

"Where's Delia, her maid?" Fargo said. "Did she leave with Alexis?"

"She went everywhere Alexis did," Lund said.

"I looked for her in the room next to us, but she was gone," Serena said.

"We need to find her. She may be able to save you. She may have seen the killer."

A stout knock on the front door. The three of them glanced at each other. Fargo stood up. "I'll go see who it is."

He moved quickly through the darkened front office, banging a thigh on a desk edge and muttering all the appropriate curses for doing so. The front door had no peephole so he had to open it without knowing who would be waiting. He turned the knob with his left hand, dropped his right to his Colt.

He recognized the face right away but took a few seconds to put a name and occupation to it. A hefty bald man named Stanley Weaver in a greatcoat and red scarf. He was Lund's personal lawyer.

"What a hell of a thing," he said, crossing the threshold. He brought in the scents of cold midnight and warm whiskey. Apparently he'd been in the office often enough that he had no problem maneuvering it even without light to guide him.

"How's he doing?" he said over his shoulder.

"How would you be doing?"

"I suppose that was sort of a stupid question."

Then they were in Lund's office. Weaver nodded to Serena and walked over to the side of Lund's desk. "You want me to be your friend or your lawyer?"

"My lawyer."

"Good. Then you know you're in trouble."

"And what does my friend say?"

"Your friend says that I'm sorry about Alexis being dead. Though I've always agreed with Serena, as you know. I never trusted her. Now I need to be your lawyer again."

"What a night," Lund said, suddenly overwhelmed

by it all again. He'd be overwhelmed several times a day for a long time.

"I'm sure they've both asked if you killed her."

"Fargo did."

"I didn't have to ask him, Stan," Serena said. "I knew the answer already."

"I didn't kill her, Stan." He stared hard at the man as he spoke.

Weaver sighed. "Good. I was afraid you might have found out something that the rest of us knew a long time ago. And then killed her for it."

"I want Fargo here to help me."

Weaver looked at Fargo. "No offense, Fargo. I know you did a good job with the stage routes but I don't know that you'd be much help with this."

"I agree. That's what I was telling him."

"We need the Pinkertons. They can be here and in place within forty-eight hours."

"I don't have forty-eight hours, Stan. Tyndale has already put me on notice that he thinks I killed her. He's got it in for me because he knows I'm going to get him defeated in the next election. He's going to end his run in Reliance by getting me hanged. And don't tell me I can fire him because if you're thinking straight, you'll realize that will just make me look guilty for sure." Then: "Fargo worked with the Pinkertons a few times. He can at least start asking the questions that Tyndale won't."

Weaver still didn't look happy about it. "You know he's going to rope you into this, don't you?"

"If Dad doesn't, I will," Serena said.

"You think you can do any good, Mr. Fargo?"

Fargo noted that he'd been moved up a notch on the social scale. He was now "Mr. Fargo." "I suppose I can try. But I'm going to run into Tyndale. He isn't going to like me running my own investigation."

"You afraid of him?"

"No. But he's wearing a badge, which is more than I can say for myself."

Weaver spoke to Lund: "I ran into our esteemed

sheriff on the way over here. He'd like you and me to be in his office in ten minutes."

"He can't do that!" Serena said. "Dad needs a good night's sleep."

"Unless your dad fires him, Serena, then he has to play by the rules. The people elected Tyndale and so he's the law in Reliance."

"But he hates Dad."

Lund said, "He's right, Serena. If I'm innocent, then I shouldn't be afraid to talk to him."

"But you're exhausted, Dad. I've never seen you look like this before."

"I'll keep it as brief as possible," Weaver said. "I'll get him home as early as I can."

Lund stood up. He walked to the coat tree, lifted his duster from it, shrugged himself into it. "I'll see you at home, honey. I'll need to explain everything to the servants, anyway. They'll be worried."

He came around the desk. "I appreciate this, Fargo. I have a lot more faith in you than you do."

"I sure can't make any promises."

"I know. But you have one thing I need right now. Faith in me. You know I didn't kill my wife."

That was the trouble, Fargo thought. Right now he didn't know enough about it all to make any judgments. As far as he knew, Lund could well have murdered his wife.

Fargo nodded at the man. That was the most support he could summon.

In the street a drunken cowboy was trying to put his boot in his stirrup and mount up. This would have been funny except for the fact that the cowboy got frustrated and hit his horse on the nose and was about to do it again when Fargo reached him.

"No need for that," Fargo told him, then hit him without great force on the jaw.

The cowboy reeled.

"You didn't like that and neither did your horse."

"I fell off him and it was his fault."

"Sure it was. Now c'mon."

Fargo helped him up into the saddle but grabbed the reins before the cowboy did. He led the horse half a block down the street. "Where you takin' me?" the cowboy asked.

Fargo could see that the café was closing up for the night. The owner was turning down the lamps. Fargo tied the reins to the hitching post and said, "I'll be right back."

He hurried inside, knowing he had little time before the drunken cowboy would fall off the horse again. In a far corner he saw a young woman rising from a table and gathering up a small gray leather suitcase and an umbrella.

"I've got a cowboy out there. See him?" Fargo said to the owner.

"I see him all right. He's pretty drunk."

"He could use a couple slices of beef and a couple slices of bread and two or three cups of coffee. Big cups."

"He packin' a gun?"

"Yeah, but I'll see that he doesn't bring it in."

"Well." The fat, freckled man shrugged. "It'll take me another half hour to get closed up. Long as there's no gun I guess it won't hurt for him to sit at the counter and eat and have some coffee."

Fargo paid him. As he headed out the door, the man said, "This has been one hell of a night. Lund's wife getting herself killed."

Outside, Fargo walked up to the cowboy and grabbed his wrist. He knew the cowpoke would resist so he said, "I'll give you a choice between having the law run you in for being so drunk or sitting in the café and having some food and coffee till you're sober enough to ride back to the ranch. Which one you want?"

But there wasn't much resistance after all. The cowboy said, "No jail for me, mister. Last time I was in one I got beat up something awful."

"Sensible man. Now get down off that horse."

"I got a sore jaw. Somebody musta hit me tonight."

"Imagine that."

The cowboy would have fallen off the horse if Fargo hadn't helped steady him. He moved in a wobbly way but he managed to get down. He didn't seem to notice that the first thing Fargo did was snap his Peacemaker from his holster. He just wobbled right up on the board sidewalk and kept right on wobbling inside.

Fargo figured he'd done both the horse and the cowboy equal favors.

He waved to the café owner who waved back. The café man had to help the cowboy find the counter and sit down.

Fargo started walking toward the Reliance Hotel. Unless Tyndale had found her, Fargo figured he'd end the night by seeing if anybody at that hotel knew where Alexis' personal maid, Delia Powell, had gone.

He was a block away when he heard a muffled cry behind him. He swiveled, his Colt already drawn, to see where the cry came from. A dark shape hugged the street. He wasn't close enough to know who the person was but he did identify the gray leather suitcase as the one the young woman in the café had carried.

By the time he reached her, she was already struggling to her feet, her black cape spread across her slender body. Her baby-fine long blond hair, a victim of the wind, covered her face. She teetered backward, caught herself, stared briefly at Fargo, and then began to pitch forward.

By now he was pretty sure he knew who she was.

9

Fargo swept the woman up in his arms, reached down to grab her suitcase, and then carried her up the street to his hotel.

At this hour the clerk was asleep behind the desk and the lobby was empty. Fargo redoubled his grasp of the woman and climbed the stairs to his room.

He stretched her out on the bed, loosened her cape, and lit the lamp. He could see that she was conscious but confused.

He sat on the chair and rolled himself a smoke.

She sat up abruptly, touching thin fingers to her breast, surveying herself to make sure she still had clothes on. "I shouldn't be in your room. It's not proper."

"Alexis has been murdered, Delia. So right now I wouldn't worry too much about what's proper."

"That's easy for you to say, Mr. Fargo. You're not a lady. I can't believe any of this is happening. I wouldn't be here if I hadn't fainted. This is the third time I've fainted in the last few hours."

Even though she wasn't quite pretty, she was appealing in her odd way. He wondered if Alexis had liked her because she was such a contrast to herself.

She caught herself slouching and sat up straight. Fargo's eyes inevitably traveled to the thrust of her small breasts against the gray linen of her blouse. She flushed when she realized that he was appraising her body. "I need your word that I'm safe here with you, Mr. Fargo."

"Completely safe. And please call me Skye."

She just looked at him. Still not sure of the reason for her being here.

"Did you talk to the sheriff?"

"Yes. He's a very coarse man."

"Mind telling me what you said to him?"

"Why, I told him the truth. I told him that Alexis and her husband had had a terrible argument and that she was afraid of him and that she told me to pack things for both of us and that we took one of the buggies and came to town."

"You had the room next to hers?"

"Yes."

"Could you hear anything from her room?"

She paused. "I'm not sure if I should be talking to you."

"Why not?"

He had to admire her loyalty. The longer he watched her, the more pleasing she became. She wasn't naive but she'd managed to maintain an air of innocence in some pretty rough situations.

She surprised him. She was on her feet in less than a few seconds, glancing around for sight of her gray leather suitcase. "I ran out. I stayed away from the hotel after it happened because I didn't want to face the fact that Alexis was dead. But I'm better now. I thank you for helping me when I fainted, Mr. Fargo. But our business is finished here."

"Any idea where you'll go?"

"That isn't any of your business."

"Did you bring any money with you when you left the mansion?"

"I never had to worry about money. Alexis always brought it."

"In other words, you don't have any money. Or not much anyway."

She walked over to her suitcase, tying her cape

around her as she moved. "As I said before, Mr. Fargo, that really isn't any of your business."

"You know, sleeping on the sidewalk can get pretty cold."

He could see the worry in her eyes when she turned to him. No money, nowhere to go. He was right, but she was stubborn and didn't want him to see that he was right.

"I'd be glad to give you the bed and sleep on the floor."

"I wonder how many women you've told that one to."

He laughed gently. "Well, let's put it this way. A, I'm very tired and need to get some sleep. B, The floor is probably just about as comfortable as that mattress. And C, I hate to say this but I'm sure I can resist your feminine charms. Believe it or not."

"Well, that's a terrible thing to say." She sounded surprised and hurt.

"It probably is. But it should reassure you that you'll be safe sleeping in the bed."

She looked at her suitcase as if her last friend were about to desert her. "Do you promise, Mr. Fargo?"

"I promise."

"And no more questions. I'm tired, too."

"All I need are the names of her lovers. And if you heard any of them in her room tonight."

"I knew there was some trick to this!"

"I'm surprised you aren't more interested in finding out who killed Alexis." He reached in his pocket for the makings. "Or maybe you already know."

She gave up, then. She went over to the bed and sat down on the edge and said, "They were all there. All three of them. And Mr. Lund himself."

"So which one killed her?"

"That's where I blame myself. I went downstairs for a quick meal and when I came back she was dead."

For a weary moment he thought the case might have been solved. Maybe she hadn't told Tyndale anything useful because she didn't like him. Maybe she was going to tell Fargo, though.

Instead, she said: "I suppose you'll want the names of all three of them."

"Yes," he said. "I suppose I will."

Sheriff Tyndale's stomach had produced so much acid tonight that he found sleeping difficult. The pharmacist had given him two different medicines for his ailment but neither one of them was working.

He sat at a table in his three-room apartment above the general store. The lamplight played rough on his lined face and tired eyes. In front of him were clippings from his various law enforcement jobs over the years. He was reading these to remind himself that he'd left each of his jobs on good terms. In all six towns there had been parties for him and gifts and the appearance of all the important people telling him what a fine job he'd done. Each new town meant more responsibility and more pay. Town councils understood ambition in a man. And no hard feelings.

Reliance was the only town he'd be humiliated by, voted out of office. All because Lund, who'd hired him to be as rough as he needed to be, turned against him when his daughter and her gentrified friends got the notion that the town should be more "civilized." Imagine that: a boomtown—civilized. What a joke.

He'd buried a wife from tuberculosis, never had any children, contented himself with whores for company, and concentrated on the task of keeping a town from sliding into chaos.

For all this he had only one thing to show: his reputation. He figured that he had one more town in him after Reliance. Bigger town, bigger pay. But would there be a bigger town and bigger pay for a man who'd been tossed out of town by the voters, his reputation now dubious?

Probably not.

So there was only one way to satisfy himself now

and that was to see that Andrew Lund—high and mighty Andrew Lund—was tried and convicted for the murder of his whore wife.

That would revive his reputation. He'd be the man who'd brought down Andrew Lund, the man who'd gone up against the most powerful man in the Territory and put him on a path to the gallows.

He'd met with all three of his deputies after Lund and his lawyer had left the sheriff's office tonight. He'd told them what he wanted them to do in the morning. And he wanted it kept up all day. All day and all over town. From the wealthiest to the dregs who puked their guts up every night in the streets. He wanted everybody to know that whatever their doubts about his time in Reliance, he was not afraid of taking on the powerful when murder was involved.

By tomorrow night a torchlit mob was going to gather outside the jail screaming for the life of the man inside. The man named Andrew Lund.

10

Brett Norton's large stone mansion rested in a small valley that was surrounded on the east by sprawling foothills and on the west by a ragged stretch of limestone wall. As Fargo approached the place on his Ovaro, he searched for sight of guards who might want to dissuade uninvited visitors.

He soon found out why Norton didn't need to hire human guards. From somewhere in the pines close by the east side of the house rushed four long-haired German shepherds. They raced to within ten feet of Fargo and his stallion and began snapping and growling with a ferocity that crackled on the morning air.

One glimpse of their white, saliva-dripping teeth reminded Fargo of the one time he'd had a run-in with a trained guard dog. Short of killing trained animals, there was no way for anybody but an expert to subdue them. And Fargo was no expert.

His lake blue eyes scanned the mansion windows. Whoever was inside must be hearing the threatening, guttural sounds of the dogs. But no one appeared.

Fargo looked around for another way to reach the mansion, but even as he searched he knew it was hopeless. Wherever he went, the dogs would go.

The wine red front door of the mansion opened and a colored man in livery stepped out on to the wide stone steps.

He appeared to be in his sixties, though from this

distance Fargo couldn't be sure. The first thing he did was half shout a single word. The word sounded Indian to Fargo. The dogs stopped growling and snapping immediately. But they didn't lie down. Their bodies remained tensed, stretched like missiles poised to strike Fargo.

"And you would be wanting what, may I ask, sir?"

"I'd like to speak to Mr. Norton."

"And what would your name be, sir?"

"Skye Fargo."

"And your business?"

"I'm here about Alexis Lund being killed." Fargo wished that he was close enough to see the servant's reaction.

The man's tone didn't change at all. "I'll convey this to Mr. Norton."

"I appreciate it."

The man repeated the word he'd used earlier on the dogs. But this time it wasn't necessary to shout. The dogs immediately lay down but their bodies remained alert, their eyes watchful.

Fargo had managed to get three hours' sleep. He'd bought the primly fetching Delia Powell breakfast, then had given her money to take a room in the hotel where he was staying. He had joked that she probably wasn't used to such common lodgings. She'd surprised him by smiling, something she didn't seem to do much of. Understandable, considering that her employer had been murdered, leaving Delia basically out on the street. "I'll have to get used to it, won't I?" she'd replied.

"Unless you find another wealthy woman to work for."

She'd shaken her head. "I think I'll go into another line of work now. Maybe learn to be a teacher. I've been a servant my entire life. I'm tired of waiting on people."

"I would've been tired of that a long time ago."

"My parents did it their entire lives. They even missed how much more difficult wealthy people in England were. They sort of looked down on Americans because they were a bit more informal with their servants."

"Sound like gluttons for punishment."

She'd smiled. "That's a terrible thought but you may be right." Then, with unexpected warmth, she'd said: "I'm sorry I was so suspicious last night. You were a perfect gentleman."

"I'm almost sorry to hear that."

She had blushed. "You're kind of overwhelming, Skye. Do you know that?"

As the front door of the mansion opened again and a man he recognized from the ballroom the other night appeared in a white shirt and black trousers and carrying a Peacemaker in his right hand, Fargo wondered if Brett Norton would find him overwhelming.

"You don't have any right to be on my property. Now get out of here before I set my dogs on you."

"I've talked to a witness who will swear that she heard you in Alexis Lund's hotel room last night around the time she was murdered."

"You're lying."

Fargo was already tired of shouting back and forth across the expanse of brown grass. "Then I'll go right to Tyndale and tell him about it. I'm sure you'll be seeing him later today."

Fargo started to turn his Ovaro back in the direction of the road but Norton snapped, "Hold on, then. Ride up here and we'll talk."

"No tricks with the dogs."

Norton clapped his hands once and then spoke another of those strange words. The dark dogs rose, turned, and began peacefully trotting to the mansion. They disappeared around the side of it.

Fargo rode up to the wide steps where Norton stood. He dropped from the saddle and faced the man.

"You don't have to tell me her name." Norton's sneer was practiced and impressive. It was clear that Norton didn't think much of the rest of humanity. "Little Miss Perfect. Delia Powell. Little bitch, if you ask me. I never could understand why Alexis liked her so much. She's the one who claims I was in Alexis' room, right?"

"If you say so. The point is that you were in the room and you had a reason to kill Alexis."

Norton glanced down at the Peacemaker in his hand as if he'd just discovered it there. "I take it you're working for Andrew. From what I heard last night, Tyndale's ready to arrest him."

"Lund says he didn't kill her."

An angry laugh. "And you believe him because he's paying you to believe him. That's how this works, isn't it? Well, I'll tell you something, Fargo. Yes, I was in her room last night. She saw me when she got into town and told me to come up later. Which I did. But I didn't have any reason to kill her. She was just another woman to me. I know a number of women, Fargo, as you may have heard. I'm not bragging. I'm a bachelor and there's nothing wrong with doing a little tomcatting."

"Even when the women are married? I hear that's your favorite sport."

A smile that was even uglier than his sneer. "Forbidden fruit. That's the sweetest taste of all. And despite what the ministers like to tell you on Sundays, it's the same for women as it is for men. Men like to sniff around and so do women. I like to think I bring a little cheer into their lives. I try to make sure that it never gets serious or out of hand, and I also try to make sure that it doesn't go on too long."

"That's very decent of you."

Norton's eyes narrowed. "You've been hanging around Little Miss Perfect too long, Fargo. She's sarcastic all the time, too. Very moral about everything. Between us, if I ever got her in bed, I'd turn her into a whore. She's the kind of girl who'd want sex twenty-four hours a day once she got the taste of it."

Fargo was tired of Norton's bragging. "You claim that Alexis was just another woman to you."

"That's right. What of it?"

Fargo needed something to rattle Norton. He chose a lie. If it didn't work, then Norton would laugh at him and go back inside. "If she was just another woman to you, why did you write her letters asking her to go away with you?"

Norton's brown eyes flashed with both anger and pain. "Little Miss Perfect started reading Alexis' mail, did she?"

"It's just as likely that Alexis told her about it."

"Well, if she did, then that's one more reason I'm glad she's dead." The words came out with such angry ease that Norton himself looked as surprised by them as Fargo did. "I shouldn't have said that."

"Probably not. Especially since you were one of the last people to see her."

But his anger was still hot. "She ran me around. Two years I put up with her." He was obviously a man who had his way with women. His tone now was not only bitter but baffled. How could any woman not do what he commanded her to? He didn't seem to notice that he'd lost his swagger and composure. "I was willing to leave everything I had here and go off with her—anywhere she chose. I could have supported us the rest of our lives."

"She wouldn't go?"

"That was just it. Three or four times she said she'd go but when it came right down to it—"

"Is that what you argued about last night?"

"How do you know we argued?" Then the sneer came back and with it his contempt. "Oh, I see. Little Miss Perfect told you we argued."

"If you say so."

"Well, I don't give a damn. Yes, we did argue. I told her either she went away with me now or we could forget the whole thing."

"She doesn't sound like the type of woman who'd put up with threats."

Norton laughed. "Alexis Lund didn't put up with anything she didn't want to."

"Not even the orders she got from Lund?"

"Not hardly. She did exactly what she wanted. She just did it in such a way that he never found out."

"Well, he found out last night."

"Yes, he did. And that's why he killed her."

Fargo saw now that Norton had not only recovered his arrogance but his unwillingness to answer any more questions. He'd just go on accusing Lund of killing his wife. "Has Tyndale talked to you?"

"No. And why should he? He knows who killed her. And don't go threatening me about telling him I went up to see Alexis last night, either. No matter how hard you try, Fargo, Lund killed her and everybody knows it. Except you. And you're being paid not to know it."

Fargo hoped that before he left Reliance he got a chance to land a few good ones on this arrogant face. "I guess we're through here."

"Yes," Norton said, "I guess we are."

He went back inside without another word. When he slammed the immense wooden door, it sounded like thunder.

Deputy Clint Pierce had never tried rabble-rousing before but he found he enjoyed it.

He stood in front of mine shaft number two talking to a group of seven miners who'd just emerged into the sunlight. They were filthy from their work, sweaty even in the cool breeze. They wore caps that allowed for candlesticks to be fitted to them. As a man afraid of tight places, Pierce had no idea how anybody could work in a mine shaft. Even worse than being killed in a cave-in was the prospect of living through the cave-in and dying slowly before anybody could rescue you. The last time there'd been a cave-in Pierce had had nightmares about it for a week.

"You men know how Lund treats you. I don't have to tell you that. You asked for more money and better conditions and you didn't get either of them."

"Hell, no, we didn't." The miner who spoke wiped a spot on his cheek with his sleeve.

"Well, those rich friends of his are going to try and protect him. They know he killed his wife and you know it. But he's going to get away with it unless you help the sheriff and me."

"What happens if we help you? What happens if he goes to prison? What the hell we gonna do for a job?" The man who spoke was short and wide, and had the eyes of a jungle beast.

Sheriff Tyndale had coached Deputy Pierce, knowing this question would be asked. "They don't shut down going concerns just because somethin' happens to the top man. Tom Byrnes really runs the place day to day anyway."

The men reluctantly mumbled consent.

"And you'd know this better than I would but if Tom Byrnes was to run things"—he allowed himself a smile—"if, say, the top man was to be in prison or getting himself ready to be hanged—I'm pretty sure you'd get a much better deal from Byrnes, don't you?"

He still had some talking to do, that was for sure. Taking to the streets against your employer was a risky thing to do. But justified or not, Lund was hated by the miners. Pierce was going to finish his talk by inviting them to the Gold Nugget where the beer would be free, thanks to an arrangement Sheriff Tyndale had made with the owner there.

One of the miners turned to the others and said, "He really is a son of a bitch and if people don't speak up he'll get clean away with murder."

Deputy Clint Pierce said, "You listen to this man, fellas. You listen to him real good. A rich man like Lund getting away with murder. Now I don't think you want that, do you?"

And it was because of their sharp responses—mostly curses—that Pierce was able to relax a little.

They would indeed be in the street tonight, swarming the sheriff's office and raising sixty kinds of hell. And if things got a little out of hand . . . a lynching maybe . . .

*　　*　　*

The great lawns of the Lund mansion were empty this morning. Usually groundskeepers could be seen keeping the site clean and proper for show. Fargo had always suspected that this was the work of Alexis, her sort of pride. Lund had pride in other matters but not in displaying his wealth. He would consider that female, weak. He was more interested in money and power.

He was greeted at the front door by Serena. Her vitality and vivaciousness were not as vibrant this morning. She looked tired and drawn, older by several weary years. Even her aqua-colored dress failed to bring any luster to her china blue eyes.

"He's had a terrible night." She didn't offer any amenities, not even a hello.

"Yours couldn't have been much better."

"It's Dad we have to worry about, Skye. I can recover from this. I'm not sure he can."

The interior of the enormous home was much like the exterior this morning. Gone were the sights and sounds of servants hurrying about, sweeping, dusting, polishing, keeping the mansion ready to please the most judgmental eye. Echoing silence this morning.

"I saw our friend Norton a while ago."

"Oh, Lord. Did he say anything?"

"I got him to admit that he was in her room last night. And that they argued."

"Then he could be—"

"Yes. He could be. But right now I need more than that to convince Tyndale to leave your father alone." Fargo didn't tell her why he was here. All he said was, "I need to talk to your father, by the way."

"He's in the study." Suspicion strained her voice: "Is everything all right? You still believe he's innocent, don't you?"

Fargo wasn't sure how to answer that. But the sudden opening of a door down the long, shadowy main hall saved him from saying anything. Andrew Lund stood there and said, "I'm glad you're here, Fargo. Let's talk."

Serena took Fargo's hand and squeezed it. "This is such a nightmare," she whispered.

In the morning light, the study had a severe look, the long leather couches and leather chairs, the framed paintings, the built-in bookcases, having the cold formality of a room in a museum, one as much for display as for comfort. Only the desk reflected the state of Andrew Lund's mind. An ashtray held the butts of at least a dozen cigarettes and a fifth of bourbon held little more than an inch of liquid. Lund didn't look drunk, simply exhausted.

After they were seated, Lund behind his desk, Fargo in front of it, Lund said, "I've been trying to figure out who was angriest with her yesterday. That's why I look so bad. Because of our argument. And her walking out. That's why Tyndale's going after me. Besides hating me, I mean. Because I'm the easiest one to make a case against. Even though I didn't have a damned thing to do with it."

"You weren't even at the hotel at any time, were you?"

"No. I didn't go near it. I knew we'd get into an argument and everybody would hear it. I didn't want to put on a show for the town."

"So you made a point of not going near the place?"

Lund was about to speak, but then he realized that Fargo had, oddly enough, asked him the same question twice. "I didn't go near the hotel, Fargo. I don't know why you're pressing that."

"Somebody told me that you were there last night. That she heard you."

Fargo could see that Lund was instinctively ready to mount an angry defense. But before a syllable of bluster left his lips, he grabbed the bottle and poured its remnants into a clear glass. The clink of bottle neck on edge of glass was loud in the spacious room. But the pouring seemed to be enough for him. Once the bourbon was in the glass, he pushed the glass away.

"That damned Delia Powell."

"She was in the next room."

"Then she told you that we didn't argue. We didn't."

"You lied to me. I asked you point-blank if you'd been up there and you said no. Now I'm not sure of anything you say."

Lund waved a weary hand. "I shouldn't have lied."

"I'd go along with that."

"I wasn't thinking clearly."

"You don't sound like you're thinking very clearly now."

The eruption that was always moments away in powerful and angry men exploded in the fist that Lund slammed down on his desk. "You're damned right I'm not thinking clearly, Fargo! Would you be thinking clearly if your wife had just been murdered and everybody thought you'd done it, including the same bastard of a sheriff you'd helped put into office?"

Lund wanted sympathy. But Fargo wasn't ready to offer any yet. "I want you to admit that you were in the room last night but that you didn't murder your wife. It's too late to lie, Lund. Things are moving too fast. The killer can't hide much longer. And that includes you."

Lund snorted. "I hire you to help me and now you're interrogating me. This is all crazy. Nothing makes any sense."

Fargo didn't relent. "I want your word to me that even though you were in her room, you didn't kill her."

"I didn't kill her, Fargo."

"Did you physically hurt her in any way?"

"No. I never laid a hand on her in our years together. Never once. I was too much in love with her."

"What did you talk about last night?"

"What else? Her coming back to me. Even after I knew how unfaithful she'd been, I wanted her back. And I'm ashamed to say it because when people cross me I either write them off or try to destroy them. But with her—as pathetic as it sounds, Fargo—I still would've taken her back."

"What did she say?"

"She surprised me. She was honest. She said that she should never have married me. That she'd been tired of her life back East and thought she could escape everything she'd been through by coming out here. She said that she cared for me a great deal but that she'd never loved me. She said she hadn't loved any of the men she'd been seeing, either. And she told me who they were—Carstairs, Norton, and—God, I can't believe this—poor Jim Holmes. My God, I can't even hate him. For a sad little man like him to chase after Alexis—I feel sorry for his wife, too."

"I still need to talk to Carstairs and Holmes."

"I want to find out who killed her. I owe her that much."

Fargo knew that the next question was going to enrage Lund. He might even be fired for asking it. But he didn't trust the servants to give him an honest answer so only Lund could help him. "Do you have any idea where Serena was earlier in the evening last night?"

Lund's gaze had drifted away from Fargo but now shot back to him. But he was surprisingly composed when he spoke. "You're saying that my daughter killed her?"

"I'm not 'saying' anything. I'm asking a question."

"Well, that's ridiculous."

"That's not an answer."

"The answer is no. I don't know where she was. But I'm positive that she had nothing to do with Alexis' death." He smiled so fully that Fargo realized Lund saw this as genuinely funny. "My daughter killing somebody? Do you know how much she weighs?"

"Probably not much more than a hundred and ten pounds or so. But Alexis wasn't exactly a giant herself."

"But she'd gotten what she wanted, Fargo. Alexis had left me."

"Alexis had left you before and come back. Maybe she thought the same thing would happen this time."

Lund frowned. "Maybe we've come to the end of our little arrangement. Maybe it'd be better if I find somebody else."

"It's too late for me, Lund. Even if you fire me I'm going to keep on asking questions. Now I need to know for my own sake who killed her."

Lund's gaze narrowed. "This isn't an attempt to get more money out of me for your work, is it?"

"Now you're being ridiculous."

"Well, I can assure you that neither I nor my daughter had anything to do with Alexis' death. And the thing I hate most about all of this is that I don't even have a chance to mourn. Whatever suspicions you have, Fargo, I loved Alexis. This is something I'd never say to Serena because she'd never forgive me for it—but I loved Alexis far more than I loved her mother."

And maybe Serena knew that without you needing to tell her, Fargo thought.

"In other words, Fargo, I still want you to find her killer even though you're wasting your time thinking that either Serena or I had anything to do with it."

Fargo stood up. "I wouldn't be doing my job if I didn't consider all the possibilities."

"I suppose you're right." Lund sighed. "But I still think it's damned insulting."

Fargo was a quarter mile from the Lund mansion when a pair of rifle bullets burned the air within two inches of his head. He was on a heavily wooded stretch of road that wound back to town.

Grabbing his Henry, he dropped to the ground and crouch-walked to the woods on his left. Shock needed a few seconds to be dispelled. Then, calmer, he began scanning the opposite side of the road. The shots had come from there. He quickly estimated the range of various rifles. The maximum would put the shooter somewhere near the small indentation where several trees had been cut down.

Fading back deeper into the woods, Fargo worked his way through the underbrush and the sweet-scented mixture of lodgepole pine and Douglas firs. Broken rays of sunlight lighted his way through the woods. Raccoons noted his passage with their usual merry disdain for human beings.

He moved as quietly as possible. He was sure the shooter would want another crack at him and maybe in so doing would show himself.

When he reached the point where he felt he was directly across from where the shooter was, he crouched down again and settled into watching and waiting.

Somewhere behind him he heard underbrush being trampled and crushed. On the wind, snaking its way through the dense woods, came the unmistakable smell of black bear. A hefty fellow no doubt looking for his breakfast. The bear sounded far enough away that he should be no problem.

Then everything happened quickly.

He didn't see the shooter but he certainly heard him. The man made nearly as much noise as the black bear. He was retreating.

Fargo stood up and broke into a run, smashing through the woods and breaking free to the road. By now he could hear the shooter rushing through his side of the woods. He'd no doubt have his horse nearby for a quick escape.

Fargo rushed into the timber, not caring that branches cut one of his cheeks or that he tripped into a diseased pine with enough force to damn near knock him out.

Ahead he could hear and smell a mountain stream. And then he could hear a horse neighing.

He hurried even faster.

But when he reached a narrow clearing that sloped down to the creek, he saw a man on a pinto jumping to the other side of the water and riding fast away. He was already out of the Henry's range.

But the shooter had made a bad mistake. He never should have worn the khaki uniform of the Reliance sheriff's office. Tyndale had only three deputies. The shooter wouldn't be hard to track down.

11

Banks always made Fargo nervous. Money inspired the worst in too many people. If it wasn't the rich robbing the poor, it was holdup men robbing and frequently killing innocent bank tellers.

James Holmes' bank tried very hard to resemble one of those fancy temples of money found in big cities back East. Flocked wallpaper, delicately shaped sconces, shiny linoleum floors, real mahogany wainscoting—the elements were there but the craftsmanship wasn't. Even the casual eye could see that the carpentry hadn't been equal to the materials. Fargo wondered if it bothered Holmes every time he saw it. It would have bothered Fargo.

The woman at the desk raised a pair of skeptical blue eyes, made her decision about Fargo in less than two seconds, and said, in a voice she reserved for all human beings who barely qualified as such, "Yes, may I help you, sir?" Fargo imagined that it took everything she had to get the word "sir" pushed from between those thin lips.

She was actually a pretty if somewhat overweight middle-aged woman. Her frilly white collar and wine-colored dress made her even more attractive. Too bad about those cold, wary blue eyes.

"I'd like to see Mr. Holmes, please."

"May I ask what this is about, sir?"

"It's personal."

"I see. Do you know Mr. Holmes, sir?"

"I don't. But my employer does. Mr. Andrew Lund."

He'd just had the only satisfaction he was going to get from this woman. That little head jerk of hers when he mentioned the name Lund. Yesterday the name Lund had meant power and obeisance. Today the name meant something else—murder and scandal. She was confused about how to react. And this was a woman who did not appreciate being confused about anything.

"I see." She seemed momentarily paralyzed.

"So I'd appreciate it if you'd go tell Mr. Holmes I'd like to see him."

The thin lips grew thinner, the eyes warier. She half whispered something Fargo didn't quite hear. She rose, pushing her dress down at the hips, and walked back to one of two offices at the rear of the bank.

While he waited, Fargo looked around. Dime novels were filled with the derring-do of bank robbers. Most of them were cast as villains but a few of them became heroes to some of the more cynical journalists and writers. Robin Hoods. That was how they were always portrayed. The trouble was, Fargo had never seen any evidence that they gave any of the loot to the needy. And even worse, the people they killed were common people just putting in their hours at the bank.

The woman came only halfway back to her desk. She raised an imperious hand and summoned him to her. When he got there, she said, "He's very busy. He can only see you for five minutes."

"How about six?" His light tone displeased her even more than his mere presence. Not that he gave a damn. "The name's Fargo, by the way."

She led him to the door, knocked lightly with a single knuckle. A man's voice said, "Come in."

She stood aside and let Fargo go in.

In a nervous, apprehensive way, Holmes was a dapper little man, Fargo supposed. The gray suit coat, black vest, and white shirt with the paisley cravat were stylish enough. The slightly graying hair gave him an air of maturity. But you always came back to that sense that he was uncertain, too eager to please, like a puppy begging for time with the master. Not the sort of qualities you wanted in your banker.

Fargo closed the door behind him. Holmes pointed to a chair in front of his desk. He'd neither stood up nor offered his hand. His walls were filled with framed citations and awards, all of them meant to convince the world—and probably Holmes himself—that he really was an important man.

"I don't have much time."

"That's what your secretary said. My name's Fargo."

"So what can I do for you?" A weak man sounding brisk in order to make himself sound strong.

"Tell me if you were in Alexis Lund's hotel room last night."

"That's ridiculous. Why would I have been in her room last night?"

Another lie. Fargo was getting good at this. "Because somebody saw you sneaking up the back steps."

"Then they saw somebody else because it certainly wasn't me." He sat back, steepling his fingers. Now he was going to pretend to relax, assess Fargo, and find him, as his secretary did, lacking. "You work for Andrew—isn't that right?"

Fargo nodded.

"Then it makes sense."

"What makes sense?"

"That he'd try to make somebody else look guilty."

"So you had no interest in Alexis?"

"Not any more interest than I have in the wives of my other friends." He leaned forward. He was feeling more self-confident. "Andrew Lund is one of my best friends. I'm not saying that I didn't find Alexis attractive, but what man didn't? I'll even admit to a passing crush on her a while back.

"That would've been—oh, two, three years ago, I suppose. She was the belle of the ball, something new in Reliance. And I was hardly alone. When Andrew wasn't around most of us talked about what she must be like as a lover. Again, who wouldn't? How many times in your life—at least out here—do you see a woman who looks like Alexis?"

"Looked. She's dead."

"All right, looked. And I'm sorry she's dead. Believe it or not, I got along with her very well. And before you read anything into that, what I mean to say is that she was nice enough to tell me that she considered me the most intelligent man in town. And that she enjoyed my company."

Fargo would have been more impressed with the performance if the little man hadn't developed a tic under his right eye; if his face wasn't suddenly shiny with sweat; and if his right hand wasn't twitching every thirty seconds or so.

"So you weren't in her room last night?"

"As I told you, that's ridiculous."

"You were home then?"

"I'm only answering these questions because Andrew is my friend—even if he did kill his wife. And it certainly looks as if he did."

"Then you were at home last night?"

"Well, no. Not till later. I had other business."

"Doesn't sound like you want to tell me what it was."

"Well, it wasn't killing Alexis—that's for sure." The tic had become more pronounced. "The other business I had was here. But I don't want anybody to know."

"Why would that be a secret?"

"Because I suspect one of the tellers of embezzling. Not a great deal of money. But money's money and embezzlers are embezzlers. I spent several hours here going over the books. Going over and over them, in fact. I want to make sure that I can prove my suspicions before I accuse him of anything."

"And then you went straight home?"

Holmes pushed back in the chair and stood up. "I've given you more time than you deserve, Mr. Fargo. And as I say, I'm doing it only because Andrew's my friend. On the off chance that he didn't kill Alexis, I don't blame him for wanting to know where his friends were. He obviously knew that we were all smitten with her at various times. He probably thinks it's worth having us questioned. But now I need to get back to work. Good day, Mr. Fargo."

Fargo bid him good day. Just before he left, he took one more look at the man. Unlikely as it seemed, Holmes being small and weak-looking, Fargo could easily imagine him stabbing Alexis Lund.

They came for Lund a few minutes before two o'clock that afternoon.

Accompanying Sheriff Tyndale were two of his deputies who were dispatched respectively to the side and the rear of the Lund mansion where there were exits. Tyndale, in his best blue suit, best white shirt, new white Stetson, and recently cleaned and oiled Peacemaker, approached the front door.

The wind was still under the impression that it was March, fierce and cold, none of the soft warmth people could reasonably expect this late in April. While he waited for an answer, Tyndale noted the way the lodgepole pines were batted back and forth as if they were little more than toys. Then he turned back to the door and wondered idly what it would be like to live in a place like this. He was impatient now. He knocked again, much harder this time. And after using his hand to knock, he slid it into his pocket and withdrew the handcuffs. He decided to play a little game with Lund. See how long it took for Lund to say something about the cuffs. See how long it took him before he realized that he was going to be arrested.

A lanky maid in a gray uniform and cap answered the door. She was properly shocked when she saw Tyndale standing there. She understood that the presence of a lawman at this time could not be good news for Mr. Lund. She'd been in town to the general store this morning, and already many of the people had decided that Mr. Lund had murdered his wife. Not that all of them blamed him; some even sympathized—her haughtiness had been a bitter joke to many townspeople—but still and all, whatever his reasons, he was in their eyes a murderer.

"I'd like to see Mr. Lund."

She was one of those liars who gulped a bit before she lied. Over his decades as a man who wore a badge, Tyndale had seen every kind of liar the good Lord had ever created, and he knew all the signs. This maid was among the worst. "I'm afraid he's asleep."

"At two o'clock in the afternoon?"

"It's all the—excitement, Sheriff. It's worn him out."

"Well, then I'll have to ask you to wake him up."

"Oh, I couldn't do that."

"I'll bet you could if I ordered you to."

"But he's asleep," she said, as if that single word should end the conversation.

He was done with niceties. "You go in there and wake him up or I will. And I'm betting that he'd rather wake up to you than me. And tell him don't bother to try and run. I've got deputies on both doors. Now do you understand what I'm telling you to do?"

"Why, I don't know why you'd say a thing like that. He's a very respectable man. And you know it."

"We believe he murdered his wife. How respectable is that?" Tyndale was never quite sure who he meant exactly when he said "we," but it sounded more imposing than a mere "I."

"Well, he most certainly didn't. You mustn't know anything about him. He loved her to the point of—"

"To the point of what?"

She was careful with her words now. "To the point of wanting to do everything to please her."

"That's probably true. Until he found out she had a few lovers around town."

The maid blushed and started to protest again. But he stopped her. "Now you go in there and wake him up—if he really is asleep, which I doubt—and bring him down here so I can talk to him. And I want this to happen pronto. Or I come in and start looking for him myself."

With that he took three long steps across the threshold, standing on the parquet floor of the vestibule, facing the winding staircase. "Now you go get him, miss. And I mean right now."

He gave himself a tour of the front hall. There was a churchlike hush to the place that made him uncomfortable. Of the twenty or so framed paintings, the only two that interested him depicted the West, a chuck wagon surrounded by cowboys and a pair of ponies running in a meadow. The others were of the sort he considered snooty. Then he came to the final painting, the one of Lund and his wife. The painter had idealized Lund. He appeared young, slimmer, more heroic somehow than he was in real life. Standing next to him in a long blue gown was Alexis. No need to idealize her. She was already about as beautiful as a woman could get.

Somewhere in the recesses of the mansion he heard Lund's voice. It was an angry voice. And it was about to get even angrier. Just a glimpse of the handcuffs would do. A man of his standing—being shown handcuffs. Let alone having to stand still while they were snapped on his wrists. The son of a bitch sold me out, Tyndale thought. Didn't have the nerve to fire me. Tricked up the election and worked behind my back for his opponent.

It was going to be a real pleasure to put these handcuffs on Lund. A real pleasure.

One minute passed. Two minutes. A silence. In a structure with such high ceilings and ornate walls, silence seemed to have echoes. No voices. No doors opening or closing. No footsteps.

What the hell was he up to?

"Lund! You'd better give yourself up!"

Echo upon echo.

"Lund! Did you hear me?"

Still, the strange silence.

"Lund!"

But he knew that shouting was useless. Lund was hiding, taunting him.

Straight ahead, the endless marble floor gleaming, lay rooms and alcoves where a man could easily hide. The servant hadn't climbed the stairs. And Lund's voice had seemed to come from the main floor. So it seemed logical to start with this museumlike hall with its paintings and statuary.

Tyndale smiled to himself when he saw the naked woman. Breasts and nipples plain to see, crotch discreetly covered with a delicate hand. In town a statue like this would incite a riot. Church ladies so old and infirm they could scarcely crawl, let alone walk, would use all their strength to take their walking sticks and smash this brazen pagan statue to jagged pieces.

Alexis would have defended this in terms of "art." Lund himself didn't know any more about art than Tyndale did. Alexis' influence. She had completely taken over the man, though Tyndale had to admit that if you had to be taken over, you might as well let it be in the arms of somebody as elegant and erotic as Alexis.

More echoes, this time of his own boots as he began to slowly work his way down the hall, his Peacemaker leading the way. The sweat came first and then the acid in his stomach. This wasn't his kind of situation. He was used to direct confrontation, not hide-and-seek.

A sound.

That was all the information his ears sent to his brain. Undifferentiated sound. Some vague resonance. It might even have come from outside.

The sound had stopped him momentarily but now he continued his way down the hall. Eyes and Peacemaker shifting side to side as he approached each door, each shallow alcove that enshrined more fancy pieces of sculpture.

The doors presented the most danger. He flung them inward, then stood aside in case Lund had decided to shoot him. So far he'd checked five doors.

The rooms, each one furnished in a fashion that looked pretentious to Tyndale, showed no signs of Lund. But flinging back each door raised the acid level in Tyndale's stomach. The acid now burned his throat. He was going to make the son of a bitch pay for this when he finally caught him.

The door he approached now had a handle different from the others, an elaborate lengthwise piece in the shape of a wolf's head. Cast in gold, of course.

He had a bad feeling about the room that lay on the other side of this door. He wasn't sure why. Maybe it was nothing more than an accumulation of his bad nerves and the searing pain of the stomach acid.

He paused, took a deep breath that he hoped would steady him. He'd find out soon enough if this was the door Lund was hiding behind.

Not until it was far too late did he become aware of a presence behind him. In a terrible second he understood two things—that Lund had been hiding in one of the rooms and that he had somehow missed finding him. And that Lund was behind him now.

As he turned, Lund dove at him with such force that Tyndale felt the Peacemaker slip from his hand. Lund rode him to the marble floor, the way he would ride a calf he was roping. Before Tyndale had a chance to even protect himself, Lund had smashed him in the head five times with one of his huge fists. Between blows Tyndale saw Lund's face. He looked insane, the eyes wild, spittle flying from the lips. He was muttering, too, curses that sounded more aggrieved than angry somehow. Insane, for sure.

Tyndale gathered himself and began to push Lund off him. But Lund swung a wild punch at Tyndale's face that managed to connect squarely on the lawman's jaw. Tyndale hadn't been knocked out in many years. But Lund had put him away long enough to disappear.

12

Two afternoons a week Serena Lund worked with the poor at Haven House, a shelter run by three nuns. Serena hadn't wanted to even get close to a job like this but her father had insisted she do it for the sake of his standing in the community. So she'd reluctantly showed up one morning six months ago to the great amusement of the sisters who worked in the four-room adobe building that the local gentry had built. They didn't often get volunteers who pulled up in expensive surreys. Nor did many of their volunteers wear clothes—costumes, really—that would have attracted attention even in Chicago or St. Louis for being costly.

Their amusement extended to watching Serena have to deal with shabbily clothed, unwashed, uneducated, and very needy men and women whose dreams and lives had gone bust when their gold prospecting had failed them. Her first afternoons at Haven House, Serena had been afraid to touch any of them. She dished their soup, she passed out their donated used clothing, she handed over the few greenbacks the nuns had been able to winnow from the wealthy—all without having any physical contact. She had turned up her very pretty nose at smells, sneezes, coughs, and other, ruder noises. She was in hell and she wasn't even dead yet.

But one afternoon the six-year-old daughter of a dead miner appeared and for the first time in her life Serena—Serena the spoiled brat—felt what mothers felt. She wanted to protect the little girl against a savage world. She became Serena's ward. In the four weeks it took for the mother to travel from Missouri to pick up the girl, Serena took her to a doctor, a dentist, a clothing store, a book store, a gift shop, and a bank. She arranged for the girl to have a trust fund of three thousand dollars. No one could touch it but the girl, and the girl could touch it only when she turned seventeen. The mother, who had been in St. Louis recovering from tuberculosis, barely recognized her daughter when she saw her.

From then on Serena Lund became the best volunteer Haven House had ever had.

She gently took the man's slender hand and turned it over so that she could see the underside of his wrist. His name was Con McKenzie and he'd left a wife and three children in Ohio a year ago to search for gold out here. Two nights ago they'd found him drunk and nearly dead in an alley.

"How're you feeling today, Con?"

He was a middle-aged man with the face of a sad hound. After a night spent in the doctor's office where it was assumed he would die, the nuns had brought him fresh clothes and told him he could stay in Haven until he was ready to go back to Ohio and face his family.

Serena's fingers gently lifted the cloth the sisters had wrapped around Con's wrist this morning. The white cloth was already discolored with green pus and dark red blood. The scabbing, the healing, was coming slowly.

"You always hear about people doin' it and it always sounds easy, the way they talk about it. I thought I did a pretty good job. 'Course, I was so drunk I guess I passed out before I got the job done right."

"Then I'm glad you passed out."

They sat on the cot where he slept. There were four cots in the cramped space of a single small room. There'd been a time when the smells of sleep, sweat, urine, and despair would have driven her from the place. But that had all changed with the little girl, Nellie.

"You still gonna help me write that letter, Miss Serena?"

"I sure am. In fact, I brought a tablet and a pencil and I thought we'd write it together this afternoon."

"She don't read too good. 'Course, neither do I."

"We'll keep it simple. I was thinking of something along the lines of 'My Dearest Margaret. I love you. I'll be home soon. Your husband, Con.' Think she could read that?"

"Well, if she can't, there's a woman lives upstairs can read it to her."

"You should have kept writing her, Con."

He smiled at her with broken gray teeth. "I didn't have you for inspiration I guess."

Serena was about to say more when Sister Felicity appeared in the doorway and said, "May I talk to you a moment, Serena?"

"Of course, Sister." The Lunds weren't Catholics so calling somebody "Sister" was still strange sometimes for Serena. "I'll be right back, Con."

Sister Felicity, a tall woman made even taller by the habit she wore, led Serena outside to the backyard where clothes on a line flapped in the wind. "One of the deputies was here. I'm afraid there's been trouble at your house."

Panic fluttered in her chest. "What happened?"

Sister Felicity took her hand. "It seems that Sheriff Tyndale went there to arrest your father but your father chose to run. The deputy told me that they'll organize a hunting party for him this afternoon. Just an hour or so from now."

Serena clutched the nun's hand. "Oh, Sister, he didn't murder my stepmother. I know he didn't."

"We'll pray very hard for him, Serena. And for you."

She needed a moment to sort through all the conflicting thoughts raging through her mind. "I need to tell Con that I'll have to write his letter for him later."

The nun let go of Serena's hand. "Right now you have more things to worry about than Con. I can help him with that letter. You do what you need to for yourself, Serena. We'll be at the church later, lighting candles for you."

Serena didn't have much faith in all the paraphernalia of the Catholic Church—she was Presbyterian—but she appreciated the nun's kindness.

"Thank you, Sister. Now I should go."

She hurried into the house for her jacket. Her horse was ground-tied at the side of the house.

All she knew for sure was that she needed to find Skye as quickly as she could.

Fargo eased himself carefully up the slope leading to Richard Carstairs' cabin.

Directly beyond the log cabin structure the mountains soared, jagged and snow-topped against a cloudless blue sky. Carstairs sat on a three-legged stool in front of his easel. Even from some distance Fargo could see that the painting was of the mountains and the sky. Carstairs was so engrossed in his work that Fargo probably could have made considerable noise without the man being aware of him.

But Fargo took no chances. He moved through the fresh mountain air with the easy skill borne of years of hunting animals and humans alike. Gray smoke curled from the chimney of the cabin; a black-and-white cow obviously used for milking stood in a small shed; a few chickens ran babbling and crazy around the back of the place.

And Carstairs, lost in his art, began to put an impressive and imposing vision of the mountains on what had been nothing more than a stretch of blank canvas.

Fargo had his Colt ready. Carstairs might have a gun on his lap. Carstairs might even be trying to fool him. Turn suddenly on Fargo and open fire.

Fargo reached a line parallel with Carstairs and began his walk to where the man sat on his stool. He stopped when he was about fifteen feet away and said, "Carstairs, put your hands up in the air."

The violent way the man jumped off his stool—stunned, shocked, terrified—revealed that he'd had no idea that anybody was sneaking up on him. He knocked over some of his paints and his brush flew out of his hand. The easel wobbled, finally fell sideways to the ground.

Seeing that Carstairs had no weapon, Fargo holstered his Colt. "I wanted to make sure you didn't have a gun."

"All right for you to have one though, huh?"

"You know who I am?"

"The one and only Fargo, from what Alexis told me. She said her husband thinks you're something special."

"When did she tell you that?"

The bravado faded quickly in the man's dark eyes. His heavy blue shirt was speckled with yellow, red, blue, green paints. He brushed a hand across his chest. A small hand, not surprising in a man so slight. He had the intensity of his craft. He didn't seem to belong in the West. "She told me who you were when you tried to sneak up here."

"Not last night in her hotel room?"

"I wasn't in her hotel room last night."

The lie came easier with every telling. "A witness saw you."

"It must've been somebody else."

"She didn't have two lovers with a limp."

Carstairs didn't respond. He stepped over and picked up the canvas that had fallen to the ground. Then he picked up the easel. His entire body jerked when he walked. When easel and canvas were righted, he turned back to Fargo and said, "All right. I was in her room. But not for long. We had a few words and I left."

"Doesn't take long to kill somebody."

"I wouldn't know. Unlike you, I've never taken a life."

"What time did you go up there?"

"Late afternoon."

"How'd you know she was staying there?"

"I saw Delia on the street. She told me."

A wind came then, stirring the pines, tilting the easel back and forth. The front door of the cabin banged shut. The chickens sounded crazier than ever.

"Anybody see you after you left her room?"

"No. I came right back here. Why?"

"Because the killer probably had blood on him."

"You're wasting your time, Fargo. I didn't kill her." He reached down by the easel and then turned back to Fargo, showing him the paintbrush he had retrieved—the symbol of his pride, the pride that had enabled him to survive in a world that did not care for creatures that were not whole and fit and like everybody else.

"You're lying, Carstairs. You know it and I know it. And this isn't finished by a long shot."

Fargo returned to the Ovaro and headed back to town.

Serena Lund stood in the middle of the afternoon street shouting up at Sheriff Harve Tyndale. The lawman was at least a full foot taller than she was. He didn't seem to be as threatened as her angry words and waggling finger wanted him to be.

Behind him, saddled up and toting rifles of several kinds, sat eleven men on horseback.

Fargo, approaching the situation, knew what he was looking at was a posse, but he wondered why it had been gathered. He dismounted and walked over to Serena and Tyndale. He heard Serena say, "Just because he ran away doesn't mean anything! It's just the strain he's under!"

He came up behind her and put a friendly hand on her shoulder. She whirled, thinking he was an enemy. She was so angry it took her a few seconds to realize that he was a friend.

"Oh, Skye!" she said. And fell into his arms.

"Good," Tyndale said. "You can take care of her. I've got a manhunt to lead."

"Wait a minute, Tyndale," Fargo said, keeping his arms around Serena, her head tucked into his chest. "Did you try and arrest Lund?"

"Hell, yes, I did. He killed his wife. I don't know where you come from, Fargo, but around here that usually means a man goes to jail. I went to his mansion all nice and peaceful and he chose to run. Knocked me out in the process."

"I'm real sorry to hear that. And as for being 'peaceful,' I'm pretty sure it was your deputy who took a shot at me when I left Lund's place yesterday."

"I suppose you can prove that."

"Yeah, about as well as you can prove that Lund killed Alexis."

"I don't give a damn about your sarcasm, Fargo. All I care about is that I've got a dangerous killer on the loose and a hysterical woman who's been pestering me the last half hour. Now get her out of my way."

He said no more. Walked back to his own horse, mounted up, and waved dramatically for his posse to follow. To Fargo they looked like most other posses— the half-drunk dregs of society eager to kill a man with legal impunity. A few of them smirked at him as they rode by. A few of them laughed among themselves. This was all a lark. They'd get out of whatever jobs they had for the day; they could get drunk on the hunt and they could come back with enough tall tales to amaze and amuse their cohorts for weeks.

Fargo helped Serena from the street and away from the curious and unforgiving gazes of the onlookers. If you couldn't watch the big and important man himself fall into public disgrace, the next best thing was to watch his daughter go all helpless.

He took her into the café, planted her in a chair, and went and got them both hot coffee. By the time he came back she'd dried her eyes, snuffled up her sniffles, and brushed her hair with her fingers. She said, almost coldly, "He wants to kill him."

He didn't answer her directly. Why make her feel worse? "Any idea where your father might go?"

"I've been trying to think of that. But I've been so damn mad I haven't been able to think clearly."

"We need to find your father before Tyndale does. And you're the only one who can help us with that."

She sat back, relaxed a bit. "He didn't kill her, Skye."

"I know."

"Are you just saying that?"

"No. I don't have any evidence of it. But it just doesn't feel right."

"How about me? You wouldn't admit it but I know you considered the possibility that I might have killed her."

"I considered everybody, Serena. That's what you have to do."

Her small, lovely face tightened again. She'd momentarily forgotten the urgency here. But no longer. "There are two possibilities that I can think of. One is an old shack near where he first discovered the gold. The other is a cave where he hid out when a tribe of Indians went on a rampage. He was with four other men and they were all killed except him. He was wounded but he dragged himself into the cave and survived. He thinks the place is almost mystical."

"Do people know about either of these places?"

"Tyndale might know about Dad's cabin. But Dad never talks about the cave much. He goes there sometimes. Like a shrine, almost. Sometimes I think he feels guilty that his life was spared but not the others'. A couple of those men were good friends of his." Then: "Does that sound like a man who'd kill a woman?"

Fargo smiled. "I believe you, Serena. No need to convert me."

"I'm sorry, Skye. I'm just so damned scared."

"All the more reason to get going and try to find him. We'd better take some supplies with us in case this goes all night. You ever slept on the ground before?"

"No. But right now I'd sleep underwater if I had to. Let's go."

Tyndale was enjoying himself. It felt good to be leading eleven men into a hunt. Some of them he'd dispatched eastward; the others he'd led to the Lund mansion in case Lund had doubled back and was hiding in the house somewhere.

As he walked around in the study, his resentment of Andrew Lund increased. Tyndale knew that he was rough with prisoners but that was due to the kind of jobs he was hired to do. You could see only so many corpses, hear so many lies, watch so many bad men get out of jail or prison and go right back to their old ways . . . seeing and hearing these things killed any possible sympathy you might have had for them.

But a man like Lund, safe and smug in a study like this, he didn't give a damn what you had to do to bring a boomtown under control. You were just his lackey. And as the town became more and more civilized, some of the gentry started to wonder if all of Tyndale's violence was necessary. Fine and dandy when he started out but now something of an embarrassment. So much so that the town council had even debated whether to introduce him to a visiting senator from Missouri. Seemed like Tyndale's reputation extended that far away.

And then not to be man enough to just fire Tyndale . . . to undermine him instead in a "fair" election. Tyndale's right hand shot out now and grabbed the neck of the brandy decanter. He hurled it across the room, smashing it into a wall filled with accolades for Lund. He enjoyed hearing the glass shatter, watching the brandy seep down over the framed tributes.

In the other parts of the house he could hear the posse members doing likewise—trashing things. He could also hear the servants crying out for them to stop. But the men only laughed and went on breaking whatever they chose. They'd no doubt be stealing

99

things, too. There might be repercussions to all this, of course, but right now Tyndale didn't give a damn.

He walked over to the massive desk and began yanking drawers out. He started hurling drawers as he'd hurled the decanter. Papers, pens, folders, rulers, stamps—the air was filled with blizzards of the stuff that had filled the drawers.

He wondered what Lund would think of all this when he came back here. But then Tyndale checked himself. Lund wouldn't have the chance to come back here. Tyndale had decided that Lund was going to die in a shoot-out. Reasonable enough, wasn't it? Man kills his wife and knocks out the lawman trying to arrest him, and then flees into the countryside? How else you going to bring a fugitive like that to justice? Everybody knew about Lund's bad temper, didn't they?

Before he left the study, Tyndale smashed two windows and took his bowie knife and carved deep lines in the surface of the expensive desk.

13

Lund's right hand was already swelling from where he'd fallen on it fifteen minutes earlier. Tyndale's horse had proved difficult to control and had bucked him off as Lund had crested a hill. The animal galloped away, leaving Lund alone with a gun hand that just might be broken. Lund had no choice but to keep moving on.

At midafternoon, the skies had turned cloudy. He could smell and taste impending rain. So damned many things on his mind it was difficult to concentrate on what he knew he needed to do. The cave. For now that was his only hope. If nothing else, he could sleep there and then try to think through everything that had happened. All he knew for sure was that he hadn't killed Alexis. But then who had? Tyndale had no interest in finding the killer. His last act in Reliance would be to disgrace and kill his onetime benefactor, Andrew Lund.

Only now, after being on the run for more than two hours, did Lund realize the mistake he'd made by knocking Tyndale out and stealing his horse and running away. If he'd turned himself over to the lawman, Tyndale would have put him in jail but Lund could have appealed to Judge Congreve and probably been freed within the hour. After all, Congreve always played Santa Claus at all the Lund Christmas parties.

But now that he was on the run . . . he'd given Tyndale the perfect chance to kill him and get away with it. Even now a liquored-up posse would be coming for him. Every man in it would want bragging rights as to who'd brought down the mighty Andrew Lund.

For a time he was disoriented. He was approaching a dark wood made even darker by the gray clouds obscuring the sun. The temperature felt as if it had dropped several degrees since he'd fled the mansion. He glanced down at his hand. It was at the point in the swelling where the skin begins to stretch like taut leather. A purple discoloration was spreading on the right edge of his thumb.

Five steps into the woods, the temperature seemed to drop even more. It was as if a door had opened and he'd stepped into a colder, darker world. He heard the chatter of a dozen different kinds of animals, smelled loam and mud and the carcasses of a myriad of creatures. The trees had just begun to bud for the spring so at least he didn't have to fight heavy foliage. But where was he exactly?

As he stumbled along a crude, winding path he had to consciously force himself to forget his aching hand. All he could worry about now was finding the cave. He'd been close to it when the horse had thrown him . . . but somehow he'd become lost.

He smelled water. Somewhere in the maze of tree and underbrush and limestone that comprised this leg of the forest, there was water. Probably a creek.

He hurried to the sudden sound of water breaking over rock. He was close by now. He would have some relief for his pulsing hand.

The creek was narrow but at least two feet deep. Its surface was covered with the dead leaves of autumn and winter. Up near its curve a moose stood with its nose ducked down into the chilly wetness.

Lund dropped down on his butt and shoved his hand into the water. It was so cold it numbed all feeling instantly. Exactly as he'd hoped.

He sat unmoving for several minutes, blanking his mind so that he could enjoy the relief the icy water had brought him. Then he had to smile. Even twenty years ago a busted hand would have been something to laugh off. He'd had a hardscrabble life for many years and pain had been part of the job. Hell, the two years he'd spent logging he'd broken a leg, an arm, and a foot. But much as he hated to admit it, his wealth had made him soft. So had age. He wasn't ancient, but he was old. And thinking of being old . . . he thought of how foolish he'd been to think that he could ever have possessed Alexis in the way he'd wanted to.

The sudden cawing of crows caused him to look up to the west. He had no idea what had incited the crows and it didn't matter. All he cared about was that he was looking at the edge of a steep cliff in the distance. A cliff edge that was familiar. Not too far from that cliff would be another deeply wooded area. And there, nestled inside heavy timber, was the cave where he had hidden from the Indians who'd been intent on killing him.

He felt a wild, unreasonable joy. The cave . . . right now it was the only home he had in the entire world. And he would be there soon. Protected.

Deputy Clint Pierce had never led men into battle before. And while this technically wasn't battle as such, it had something of the same effect on him. Exhilaration.

Plus, it was an opportunity. Come the next election, Pierce would be out of a job, at least in Reliance. The new sheriff would bring his own deputies on. Pierce could find employment in town, but after all the enemies he'd made wearing the badge he'd have no protection if he stayed around. All that would change if he brought in Andrew Lund, alive or dead. Preferably, to Pierce's way of thinking, dead. He imagined Lund thrown unceremoniously over the back of Pierce's own horse. The way people would follow him down the street, eager for a closer look at the corpse. The little ones would go crazy. He'd be as big a hero as the men in dime novels. And the merchants would probably be of a mind to forgive him for all the bills he'd run up and had yet to pay off.

He was in the midst of these thoughts when he heard the shouts behind him. Shouts and—by the time he'd turned around in his saddle—laughter.

Tyndale had sent him eastward to check out Lund's fishing cabin. Tyndale was going to hunt the hills to the west of the mansion. Pierce hadn't had any say as to which men went with him and which with Tyndale. He didn't object because he would just piss off the men he was stuck with if he pointed out that they were the worst of the lot.

But now he wished he had said something. One man was so drunk he'd fallen off his horse.

The other men had dismounted and were standing in a circle around something that was making a lot of noise. It was supposed to be a man but it didn't sound like a man, the way it was spluttering and screeching and thrashing around. But then came a sound only a human being could make. Vomiting. The son of a bitch was puking all over the place.

Harley Carnes worked for the town blacksmith. Worked, that is, when he was sober, which was less and less often these days. He'd been drunk when the posse had left town. Pierce had warned him to throw away his pint. When Carnes seemed reluctant, Pierce had grabbed it from his hand, turned it upside down, and then pitched the bottle into some nearby bushes. Then the posse had continued riding.

But obviously Harley had had another bottle stashed someplace.

"Get out of my way," Pierce snapped at the men around the fallen figure of Carnes.

They made room for him at once. They knew what was coming. It would be fun to see.

Carnes was on his hands and knees, dog style. He was so drunk his head wobbled back and forth as if it were about to fall off. His eyes were wild, unseeing. Puke dripped from his face.

The first thing Pierce did was bring up the point of

his boot with such force that he cracked two of Harley's ribs at once. The chunky man screamed and fell on his side. He made the mistake of landing with his legs spread. Pierce didn't have any trouble sending the same boot straight up into Harley's groin. He literally raised Harley a good inch off the ground. Harley was sobbing like a woman. "Please! Please! Don't hurt me no more, Clint! Please!"

Even the others looked warily at each other. Slapping Harley around some, that was understandable. Leaving him out here to freeze his ass off till he sobered up, that was understandable, too. But this—

The next thing Pierce did was walk up the length of the man till he was at the grizzled head. He raised his boot, hesitated, raised his eyes to meet the apprehensive gazes of the posse, and then delivered the point of his boot to the side of Harley's head with enough force to elicit a groan that had the sound of death to it.

"You killed him!" one of the men shouted.

"No, I didn't, Gaither. But I should have. And the next man to take a drink is gonna get the same treatment." He spat. "Or worse."

The fishing cabin hadn't been used for some time, long enough that a number of small animals had found various ways in and had used it as both a shelter and an outhouse.

Because there were only two large rooms and a small native stone fireplace, it didn't take Fargo and Serena long to see that her father wasn't here. And from what they could find, hadn't been here.

They stood outside. The threat of rain was heavy on the air. The river before them ruffled with the wind.

The cabin sat in a cul-de-sac of pine trees. A long stretch of shale led to the water. Fargo figured that this would be an ideal place for men who wanted to get away from work and the burdens of being a good citizen.

"The cave," Serena said. "I can't think of any other place."

Fargo was about to say something, but to the west he heard the sound of approaching horses. The riders were coming fast.

"Do you hear something?"

"Be quiet."

He tried to gauge how much time it would take them to arrive at their present speed. He couldn't be sure but if they didn't have to stop for any reason, they'd be here within fifteen minutes or so. There was a good road leading very close here. They were making good time.

"We'd better go. I'm pretty sure that'll be part of the posse."

"I just can't believe it, Skye. My father hunted down like some animal."

He didn't want her to give in to herself. She was tough but she was emotional. He took her hand and led her to the horses.

They'd traveled less than a quarter mile when the icy, slashing rains came. They'd both donned their ponchos. They sank down inside them. He followed her directions. This was her territory.

The wind broke branches in half, the rain turned ground into mud dangerous for horses, and vision was limited to no more than ten yards ahead. Several times her horse balked, started to stumble. But she knew what she was doing. She steadied the animal and plodded on.

The wind doubled, perhaps even tripled in force and Fargo knew they'd have to stop for a while. His eyes began searching the narrow trail for some sort of resting place.

"Skye, I think I have to stop," she said, her words fragmented by the tearing wind.

He nodded to a short span of forest. There had been many nights when he'd had to fashion himself a makeshift shelter to hold off the worst of rain or snow. This was another one of those situations.

He waved in the direction of the forest and set off.

He rode slowly, carefully. It was full dark now and risky to take an animal very fast over such terrain. Every minute or so he'd look over his shoulder to make sure that she was still behind him. Given the fury of the wind he wasn't sure he'd hear her if something happened to her horse.

They dismounted when they were still several feet from the line of trees. They grabbed the reins and guided their mounts into the forest. There was enough foliage at the tops of the trees to make a noticeable difference in the intensity of both the rainfall and the winds. They still chilled them but their power had been reduced appreciably.

The deeper they penetrated the darkness, the more heavy pines they found. And beneath the heaviest of the pines they found a reasonably dry place to sit.

After a few attempts, Fargo was able to build a small fire. Jerky and bread were the only items on the menu. In the light of the flames Serena looked like a very wet child, her big blue eyes filled with apprehension and disbelief that any of this was happening to her.

"I'm just worried that they'll get to the cave before we do, Skye."

Thunder rumbled across the sky they could no longer see. Then ragged pieces of lightning illuminated the darkness above them. And the rain slashed down even more furiously.

"They'll be holed up the same way we are. They can't travel in this, either. And we don't know for sure that they know anything about the cave."

"I'm just afraid that if they catch him before we do—"

Their hats and ponchos had kept them dry enough to sleep without feeling like they were drowning. But when Fargo suggested that they try to sleep for a while Serena was shocked, almost angry. "My father's life is at stake. And you expect me to sleep?"

He had to gentle her down. "Serena, one thing I've learned is that if you can grab fifteen minutes of sleep

107

here and there, you're usually stronger for it. We don't know what's ahead. A little sleep will help both of us. I learned that a long time ago. You can go thirty-six, even forty-eight hours without going to bed if you take little sleep breaks."

He'd been thinking of other ways to spend their time here in the woods. His eyes kept automatically resting on her thrusting breasts and the sweet curves of her riding breeches. But he had to restrain himself for her sake. She was single-minded at this time and she was right to be. As she'd said, her father's life was at stake.

Fargo sat with his back against a thick pine. The brim of his hat was wide enough to keep the occasional raindrops from dousing the cigarette he'd built for himself.

Despite her best intentions to stay awake, alert, Serena yawned. And then smiled. "I didn't realize how tired I was until you brought it up, I guess."

"You've been through a lot in the last twenty-four hours. It's bound to wear you out."

She yawned again. "But I feel guilty even thinking about myself. Think of what my dad's going through." When she yawned a third time she broke into a reluctant smile. "I see what you mean about taking little naps. I'll bet I could use one right now."

She'd been sitting next to him, trying to stay close to the warmth of the small fire. The steady drone of the rain, the sweet smell of the pine, and the silky feel of the needles beneath them made her feel as if they were in a cave of their own. She eased herself closer to Fargo, so close that she could rest her head on his shoulder. She needed to feel protected now, as if there were a force in the world that could right the wrongs that had been put in her way. She wanted to be a little girl again, the daughter of Andrew Lund, the man who could do anything. But now Andrew Lund was an animal scurrying through the torrents of night and storm, fleeing for his life.

Fargo sensed all this in her. He slid his arm around

her and drew her near. With his fingers he angled her hat so that it covered her eyes. She muttered a dozy thank-you. It wasn't long before she was asleep there in the protective curve of his arm. Tiny snoring issued from her lips. He smiled at the sound.

Fargo finished his cigarette and then tilted his own hat down across his eyes and fell asleep himself.

A full moon guided them across a landscape gleaming from the recent rain. Even the wind had abated and the night was still and solemn except for the coyote cries that came on occasion. The snow on the mountaintops glowed silver and serene.

Fargo had slept longer than he'd planned to. His arm was a little stiff from where he'd held Serena for so long but otherwise the shut-eye had reinvigorated him.

They had been traveling two hours. Serena said that they were close to the cave. She'd chattered a lot on waking but had now slipped into nervous silence. Fargo figured she was probably imagining all the worst possibilities for her father.

"The cliff!" she said.

Fargo raised his eyes to see a narrow, protruding shelf of rock on the edge of a cliff. The protrusion was almost like a finger about to beckon travelers. A landmark for sure.

"There's a trail we pick up in about a quarter mile. The cave's down in a wooded area."

Fargo hadn't seen her this happy since he'd first met her the night of the party. He knew she wouldn't be happy long, not with what he had in mind. In fact, she was likely to see him as a traitor, hate him.

They were soon guiding their horses onto the trail she'd talked about, slowly climbing the side of the cliff. Her excitement was almost amusing. She was under the impression that just seeing her father would make everything all right. That just holding him would banish all the other problems and they could go back to their normal lives.

They ground-tied their horses at the top of the cliff and proceeded on foot down the steeply sloping ground to the wooded area. Fargo brought his Henry along, which seemed to bother Serena. She didn't say anything but she looked surprised and annoyed when he hefted it before they started walking.

A good thing Serena knew where the cave was. Otherwise Fargo would have spent an hour searching for it. They had to wend and wind their way through closely grouped hardwoods and then work their way carefully down the side of a shallow but rocky gulley. Even then, in the broken moonlight, the cave was hidden behind underbrush, its opening so small that the eye could easily miss it.

She screamed.

She'd seen her father before Fargo had.

Andrew Lund had not quite made it to the cave. He'd fallen into deep underbrush to the side of it. He lay facedown and Fargo's first impression was that Lund was dead.

Serena threw herself to the ground next to him. Fargo was close behind her, watching as she began to turn him over so that they could see his face. The first obvious sign of what had felled Lund was the long bloody gash across his forehead.

"Dad! Dad!"

Fargo took off his poncho and spread it out on the ground. Then he turned to Serena. "Let me in there." At first she was unwilling to let go of her father but Fargo's hands were insistent. He helped her to her feet and then bent down and struggled to get a grip under Lund's body.

Given the length and weight of the man, Fargo had to struggle some to carry him into a section of moonlight. Serena had brought her canteen. The first thing Fargo did was take it from her and gently raise Lund's head so that he could drink. Lund muttered something delirious. At first he didn't open his lips and the water trickled down his chin. Fargo pressed the canteen to

Lund's mouth. This time Lund drank, though only a few drops.

Serena said, "Look at his hand."

From a brief glimpse Fargo could see that Lund's right hand had been broken in at least two places. The bruising was ugly, the swelling even uglier.

For the next half hour they gradually brought him back to shaky life. His breathing eventually became normal. He'd been wheezing badly when they'd first gotten his eyes open. He drank increasing amounts of water and Fargo was able to prop him up against a nearby tree.

At one point Serena babbled. "We'll go to Europe, Dad. You'll never get a fair trial here. You've always wanted to see Europe. We'll live there the rest of our lives. I know you can figure out a way to get enough money for us. And if I need to, I'll work. I won't mind it at all. Whenever we go to Chicago I always think about how nice it would be to work in one of those fancy dress shops. I could make enough for us to live on. And we'd be safe. And everything would work out for us."

If Lund heard her, he showed no indication of it. He stared off into the dark distance. Serena took off her poncho and laid it across Lund's shoulders and chest. Fargo got a fire going and asked her to go back and get coffee from the saddlebags.

The fire and the coffee stirred Lund for the first time. Fargo checked the gash in his forehead and then his hand. "You remember how you got either of these?"

Lund's voice was weak. "I fell on my hand when Tyndale's horse bucked me off. The head—I slipped on something while I was climbing up here. I think I was out for a while. It took some time for me to remember anything. I couldn't figure out what I was doing out here. I remembered who I was but that was about all."

"Oh, Dad. This is so terrible. This is all because of Tyndale."

Fargo said, "Tyndale's got it in for you, no doubt about that. But he's also doing his job."

"Don't even say that, Skye!" Serena snapped. In the firelight her face looked fierce, a warrior princess defending her father.

Lund said, "I expect he's right, honey. It was foolish of me to run. That only gave Tyndale more ways to convince people I was guilty. I should've let him take me in."

"How do you feel about that now?" Fargo said.

"He's not going to turn himself in," Serena said.

"It's the only way to handle it, Serena," Fargo said as quietly as possible. "And I think your father knows that now."

"Trust him to Tyndale? I'll never let that happen, Skye. I promise you that."

Lund said, "I need to go back, honey. I should get a lawyer in from Denver and I should go through the legal process."

"And I'd send for some Pinkertons," Fargo said.

Lund winced. Touched his good hand to the slash across his head. "You quitting me, Fargo?"

"No. But having some real detectives helping you sure won't hurt."

"This is crazy, Skye. Tyndale hates Father. He'll do anything he can to see him hang."

"There's no other choice, Serena. I'm sorry, honey. You'll just have to accept it. I can't run. I never should have given in to panic the way I did. I need to see a doctor. I'm in a lot of pain and it's not helping me being out here in the cold and rain."

"But Europe—"

For the first time, Lund laughed. "You don't really think your old man would fit in with all those European dandies, do you? And you working in a dress shop? The first time somebody gave you an order you didn't like, you'd tell her off and storm out."

The anger remained on Serena's sweet face for only a moment. Then she not only smiled but laughed. "I guess it is pretty difficult to imagine you in a drawing

112

room discussing art and music with a bunch of Frenchmen." Then: "Or the spoiled princess lasting very long in a dress shop." She touched Fargo's arm. "We need to protect him, though, Skye. We need to make sure that Tyndale doesn't hurt him."

"I'll make sure of that."

"Your word of honor?"

"She's been saying that since she was three years old, Fargo. You'd better give her your word of honor."

"My word of honor."

"There," Lund said, "maybe she'll stop pestering you for a while."

14

Not even Deputy Pierce's violent temper could turn the remaining members of his posse back into the angry men who lusted after the life of Andrew Lund. What Pierce was dealing with now was a mutiny. The long night's rain and cold had sobered the men up and they sat their saddles now in damp clothes and sullen refusals to obey any of his orders. As one of them said: "Why don't you arrest me and take me back to town? I'd rather be in a cell than out here freezing my ass off." As if to underscore his point, he sneezed.

They were headed back to town.

Pierce pretended that the terrible drenching night hadn't affected him. He still rode point, sitting his saddle tall and formal, like a West Point man leading his first troop in Injun country.

The men mumbled and grumbled among themselves. These were town men given to big talk in saloons but without the necessary experience or mental stamina to persevere in rough country—at least not when they were sober.

They crossed a wide creek and headed up a steep slope to a plateau that was just beginning to bloom with buffalo grass. In the distance they could see a Conestoga wagon rattling across the prairie, headed for Reliance. It would be packed with everything the family owned. But there would still be plenty of room for the dreams the man had and the doubts his wife had brought along. The children would be excited even though they'd had to endure numerous hardships on their travels.

A few minutes later something nagged at the corner of Pierce's right eye. He turned his head to see what it was. At first he refused to believe what he saw. Things didn't happen this way. Just fall out of the sky and right into your lap. No, sir.

He reached back to grab his field glasses from his saddlebag. He brought them to his eyes. And damned if what he'd thought impossible was not only possible but real.

Big as you please, coming down a sloping Indian trail, were Fargo and Andrew and Serena Lund. Lund was slumped in his saddle. A terrible wound stretched across most of his forehead. Serena rode close beside her father, looking to grab him if he started to fall out of his saddle. They were obviously headed back to town.

As yet the posse behind him hadn't noticed the three. They were too busy bitching about Pierce.

Despite his weariness, Pierce began to formulate his plan. There was still time to be the hero here, still time to secure his job with the new sheriff. Still time to be the man who captured the most prominent fugitive in the history of Reliance.

He turned his horse back to the men and ordered them to halt.

"If you look to the east, you'll see three people riding toward town."

Grizzled, tired, cranky, the men followed the line Pierce's arm pointed out. "I used my field glasses. That's Lund and his daughter and Fargo."

The reaction wasn't jubilation but for the first time since sunup the men showed interest in something other than bitching and getting back to town. "Wish to hell we'd spotted them yesterday," one of the men groused. Then: "But what the hell? We'll have us some fun now, I guess."

"It's not too late. I'm the law here, not Fargo. And

me and my posse, we're the ones who should be bringing Lund in."

"Damn right," a man said. "We was sworn in all
official and everything. Fargo wasn't."

Deputy Pierce wanted to have some fun with them,
work them up. "But I imagine you men want to head
back to town, and I don't blame you. So you go on
and I'll ride over there and take charge of Lund."

"Hell, no," two men said at the same time. One
of them grinned. "There's liable to be some shootin',
knowin' Fargo and all. Why should you get to have
all the fun?"

Pierce smiled. "You mean you'd rather ride over
there and maybe have to do a little gunplay than head
back to town right away?"

"I always hated Lund. I just hope he tries to run
again."

"I wouldn't mind takin' that Serena in the woods
and showin' her that big surprise I got for all the
ladies."

"Time I slept with your wife, she told me my surprise was a lot bigger than yours."

The men laughed. Gone was the discomfort with
wet clothes, sore throats, hungry bellies. Hell, none of
that mattered, not with the prospect of some shooting,
it didn't.

"Let's go," Pierce said.

"Dad really needs to get to a doctor, Skye."

Even though Lund hadn't said anything for a while,
even though he looked as if he might drop right off
his saddle, he summoned enough strength to make a
joke: "Honey, I think Fargo's going to get real sick of
hearing you say that. I'm getting a little sick of it, too."

Serena was surprised. "Have I been saying that a
lot?"

"No more than five or six times in the last ten minutes," Fargo said, laughing.

"Oh, Lord, I'm sorry. I'm just so worried—"

"Relax as much as you can," Fargo said. "We'll be

in town in another hour or so. We'll go straight to the doctor's. Then I'll try to round up Tyndale and bring him to the doc's."

"He won't like it that you don't bring Dad to the jail first."

"Well, right now I don't care much what Tyndale likes or dislikes. Do you?"

She shook her head, bitterness flashing in her eyes.

They were on the stage road. The sun was warming the morning and Fargo was feeling good that they'd found Lund before the posse had.

A few minutes later he had to qualify what he'd been thinking because coming at them, riding hard, was a group of men that could only be one part of the posse. Tyndale had likely split his men in two.

"Who's that, Skye?" Serena said, fear on her face and in her voice.

"Looks like the posse. Or part of it."

"But we're taking Dad back. We don't need them."

Fargo's hand covered his Colt. "Looks like we're going to get them whether we want them or not."

Well, if nothing else, Fargo thought as the posse rode up, they looked a lot more sober than most posses he'd seen. A night in cold rain has a restraining effect on a man. Especially if he's run out of liquor.

Deputy Pierce rode up front. In town he put on an amiable face, playing the reasonable, humble lawman to Tyndale's angry, implacable sheriff. But out here he got to live out his dime-novel daydreams. The way he rode this morning was military style, his men behind him, obeying the signals he gave with his arm.

"Morning, Fargo."

Fargo nodded. "We're taking Mr. Lund back to town."

"Well, I appreciate your efforts, Fargo, but since I'm the one with the badge, I'll have to ask you to turn him over to me right here and now."

"No!" Serena cried.

"I think we'll just keep on heading in the way we

have been," Fargo said. "We're close to town and Lund here needs a doc. We'll take him straight to Doc Standish's office and then you can put him in custody."

The men behind Pierce grumbled, making it clear what the plan was. Lund was to be turned over to them. They'd be men with grudges, of course. A rich man makes a lot of enemies and right now Fargo was looking at several of them.

"Afraid it's not going to work that way, Fargo. I want him turned over to me right now. I know you're fast with a gun and all but you're not fast enough to take on all of us."

"Don't let them take Dad, Skye."

"You want the glory—is that it, Pierce?"

"Just doin' my job is all, Fargo." Pierce then dropped from his horse. He tugged up his leather gloves and started walking toward Lund.

Fargo slipped off his Ovaro, too, took four quick steps, and blocked Pierce's path. "Serena and I found him, Pierce. Why don't you make this easy for everybody and let us take him in?"

" 'Fraid it's not gonna work that way, Fargo. Now get out of my way."

Somehow Serena was there. She lunged in front of Fargo and pushed at Pierce's chest. He was quicker and stronger than Fargo would have thought. He turned her completely around and shoved her back into Fargo. He started to reach for his gun. Fargo knew that any kind of crossfire was likely to wound if not kill Serena, who was staggering in front of him, trying to right herself.

Now it was Fargo's turn to shove her. He pushed her with such force that she stumbled at least four feet away. Even though Pierce drew first, Fargo's bullets tore into the deputy's shoulder and arm.

He'd moved so quickly that Pierce's first reaction was surprise more than pain. He'd never seen anybody who could be that fast and that accurate at the same time. His own bullets had gone wild.

As Pierce started to sink to the ground, one of the men in the posse took at Fargo with his rifle. Fargo's bullets lifted the man's greasy hair from his head with such bloody ease that the man looked as if he'd been scalped. He went over backward off his horse but one of his boots caught in a stirrup, and the horse, spooked, started dragging him across the prairie at high speed. The man was lucky he was dead.

Then another man, who apparently thought he was out of pistol range, raised his rifle and took a bullet in the chest for his trouble. He fell facedown on his horse, blood coming in puked-up torrents. Then he fell, slamming into the ground.

Fargo faced the other men, moving his Colt back and forth, ready to kill all of them if necessary. "I want all your weapons thrown on the ground now."

Only one of them, a man with a white beard and a smashed-in face, hesitated, obviously weighing his chances of surviving a gunfight with Fargo. Seeing this, the man sitting on the next horse said, "You got that new granddaughter, Owens. You're always braggin' on her. You draw down on Fargo here, you'll never see her again."

Owens wanted to demonstrate that even though he wasn't going to fight he was still a tough, scary bastard. He conjured up his meanest snarl, spat on the ground, and said, "You just shot a lawman. You're in big trouble, Fargo."

"You let me worry about that. Now two of you get over here and pick up the dead one and toss him on his horse. Then patch up Pierce as well as you can and take them all back to town."

Pierce was moaning. He was speaking nonsense. Sometimes he sobbed. Shock and blood loss were taking their toll. He'd wet himself and his right hand twitched violently. Serena stared at him and then swung her eyes away. Even if she hated him, seeing him like this was pretty ugly.

The men pitched their guns and rifles and then climbed down off their horses. One of them sobbed when they picked up the dead man. The other man, the one with the white beard, called Fargo several names, making sure that Fargo heard each of them. They tied the man to his horse and saddle.

Pierce was more of a problem. They had to put him up in his saddle and tie his hands to the horn. He seemed to go in and out of consciousness. They then decided to tie his ankles to the stirrups.

"You'll regret this, Fargo," the white-bearded one said when they were mounted again and ready to go.

"Pierce needs a doc pretty bad. You better head out."

A parting snarl, more curses and dirty names. Then the group of them swung their mounts toward town and set off. Pierce looked like a dead man somebody had strapped upright as a joke.

Serena sat next to her father, helping him to drink from the canteen. There wasn't much water left. She wanted to make sure none of it spilled.

"I see why so many men are afraid of you, Skye," Andrew Lund said. As far as Fargo could figure, this was the first time Lund had ever used Fargo's first name.

Fargo shrugged. "Looked a lot more impressive than it was. Pierce is no gunny and those men took way too long to try and kill me. They should've shot me about the time I was firing on Pierce. There was a lot of luck involved."

People stood on either side of the street watching as Fargo, Serena, and Lund made their way slowly to Doc Standish's office. Some of them yelled for others to come and see, too; some just stood silent, like sentries; and some shook their fists at Lund and shouted names at him. Wasn't often you got to scream insults at the most powerful man in the Territory and get away with it. This was a special day.

Every few feet somebody would lunge out of line at Fargo. He could push most of them back with just a scowl. Not even being part of a mob could make all men brave. A woman spit at him but her aim was off. Serena shouted at her. A few times Lund's head lolled to the right as if he'd passed out. But then he'd jerk awake and gape around as if he wasn't quite sure where he was or what was going on.

Serena rushed into the doc's office while Fargo tied their horses to the hitching post and then helped ease Lund to the ground. Fargo carried Lund inside. Serena was talking anxiously to the doctor.

"I'm just worried he's not going to make it, Doctor."

"Well, Serena, he's not going to make it if we all stand around here and just worry ourselves to death. Now you take some deep breaths and force yourself to calm down. You're not helping anybody acting the way you are." His words were not unkind. He meant to help her and it was clear she realized this. She put a hand on his arm and nodded.

He led them into his examination room. The first thing he did was turn up two large lamps. The second thing he did was grab his black leather medical bag. The third thing he did was go over to the window and raise the shade. Sunbeams filled the room. The doctor required a lot of light.

"Just lay him down real gentle," the doctor said to Fargo. For all that he'd told Serena to relax, Fargo could see a brief bit of panic in the medical man's eyes when he started looking closely at Lund.

Fargo and Serena eased Lund back on the examination table. Lund's eyelids fluttered but Fargo wasn't sure the man was truly conscious.

"Now I need you to tell me what happened to him while I'm looking him over," the doctor said. "And I need you to tell me real slow and real easy. And don't get yourself excited while you're doing it."

He was obviously talking to Serena. She told him everything in careful terms, as unemotionally as possible given the circumstances. As she spoke, the doctor began a careful examination of the big man on the table.

"Fine," he said when Serena was finished talking. "Now you two go wait in the other room. There're some nice, comfortable chairs there for you to sit on."

Serena hesitated, didn't want to leave her father's side, but the doctor's frown was persuasive.

Serena sat on the edge of a wooden chair. Fargo remained standing. "I need to go talk to Tyndale. If he's back."

She clutched his wrist. "I don't want to turn Dad over to Tyndale, Skye. I'm just afraid."

Fargo patted her hand. "We don't have any choice. Even if your dad wanted to fire him now, he couldn't. The town council wouldn't go along with him. They couldn't afford to. Too many people think he's guilty."

"But to be in a jail cell . . ."

Fargo shook his head. "Your dad's too sick for a jail cell. He'll have to stay here under guard."

"You really think Tyndale will go along with that?"

"We brought your father in. That was our part of the bargain. Now he has to make his part. He can't take care of your father in jail. Only the doc can do that. And that means your father stays here."

Serena's worry creased her forehead. Amazing that after all they'd been through her vibrant good looks still managed to shine. "I'll just wait here, then. I just hope Doc Standish doesn't find anything else wrong with him."

"Standish knows what he's doing, Serena. Now I need to go."

He was a celebrity on the street. Eyes from windows, from sidewalks, from wagons, horseback, surreys, and even a stagecoach followed his block-long walk from the doc's to the jail where a crowd of maybe twenty people stood in the street, talking among themselves. When one of them spotted Fargo, they all turned to glower at him. He was the enemy. The drifter who was protecting the rich killer. Whatever misgivings they'd had about Tyndale were gone now. He was the hero. Lund and his protector were the villains.

"Where's Lund?" one of the older women snapped at him. In her gingham bonnet and gingham gown, she should have looked female and motherly. But something happened to meek people when they became part of mobs, even just a tiny one like this. They became strong in a bad way, dangerous with the strength and rage of others to draw on.

"I'm sure Tyndale will explain everything to you," Fargo said.

A young man, big and already drunk, stepped from the group and said, "She asked you a question." He was the crowd favorite, a brawler with wide shoulders, huge hands, and a scowl he must have practiced in front of a mirror since he was a little boy.

"And I answered it."

Fargo was about to look like a legend again. Putting somebody down with a single swift punch planted deep into a belly. But again, a good part of the moment was pure luck. The young man was drunk for one thing and for another, despite his size, he wasn't much of a fighter. He swung first, a wide roundhouse that Fargo easily blocked with his arm. Then Fargo slammed his fist into a point just below the solar plexus.

The young man staggered, wobbled sideways, and delivered unto the street one hell of a stream of vomit.

The crowd was quelled for the moment. Fargo pushed past them and went on into Tyndale's office.

As he crossed the threshold, Tyndale moved away from the window where he'd been watching everything. "Doesn't look like you made many friends out there, Fargo."

"Lund is over at the doc's and I want him to stay there."

Tyndale came over to his desk and sat down. He'd had the chance to shave and change clothes after his night in the rain and wind but heavy lines creased his face, and his eyes were red from lack of sleep. "What happens if I say no?"

"You won't say no because you know you can't take care of him here. He'd throw off your routine."

"I'm impressed that you're worried about my routine."

Fargo parked himself on the edge of the other desk in the front room where the walls bloomed with wanted posters and shiny glass cases for rifles. "He didn't kill his wife."

"You think maybe she committed suicide?"

"No, I think there's a good chance one of her lovers did it."

"I assume we're talking about Norton, Carstairs, and poor Jim Holmes."

"That's right."

"You have a favorite?"

"Not yet. But I hope to have one before the end of the day."

"Lund still had the best motive for killing her."

"And you've still got the best motive for pinning it on him."

Tyndale sat back, put his boots up on the desk. "Then I guess it's up to you to prove me wrong."

"I guess it is."

He stared at Fargo for several long seconds. "Lund can stay at the doc's. But now we've still got a problem, Fargo. Seems you wounded my deputy and killed two posse men."

"I didn't have any choice. Pierce wanted credit for bringing Lund in. I didn't trust him. I figured he might kill Lund to make things look better. I wouldn't hand Lund over so Pierce drew on me. And while I was fighting Pierce, the other two aimed their rifles at me and were getting ready to fire."

"You must be pretty fast."

"Pierce was slow. And he was tired. And the other two were so hungover, their timing was way off. I was defending myself and nothing more. All I wanted to do was bring Lund in. It was stupid of him to run in the first place. But now that's beside the point. I mean to find out who killed Lund's wife."

"You want to waste your time, go ahead. Far as I'm concerned the killer's in custody over to the doc's place."

Fargo moved off the desk. He walked over to the

window. The crowd was gone. "Looks like your company left."

"They'll be back. They don't like the idea of a rich man getting away with killing his wife."

Fargo walked to the door. "I'm surprised they cared that much about Alexis."

Tyndale snorted. "Care about Alexis? They hated her more than they hate Lund. Lund's just a rich man. Alexis was rich and a bitch. She had no time for the common people and she made that very clear. The shop owners wanted to close up when they saw her coming. She could never find what she was looking for and she'd insult them about it. Ridicule them. Call them stupid, things like that. One time she did it in front of a woman's little girl and the little girl started crying. You'd think that'd make Alexis back off a little. But all she did was rag on the mother about what a brat her little daughter was."

"Sorry I never got to know her."

He took his feet down from the desk, leaned forward on his elbows. "I've got it in for Lund, and you know it and I know it. I cleaned up this town for him. I'm still too rough, I suppose, since the town's calmed down some. But he didn't treat me right, Fargo, and you can believe that or not. He owed telling me face-to-face that I was through. But he didn't. He decided to go through this whole rigmarole of getting me unelected. I deserved better than that."

If that was true, Fargo thought, he had to agree with Tyndale, much as he hated to. Lund had owed Tyndale better than that.

"That still doesn't give you the right to try and hang him."

Tyndale smirked. "Well, I'm probably not going to have that pleasure with a detective like you working for him, now am I?" He laughed. "Good luck, Fargo. Just remember to stay out of my way."

Fargo wasn't fooled by the jovial comments. This was a man who hated Lund and planned to punish him.

Half a block from the sheriff's office a female voice said: "Mr. Fargo."

In the thunder and din of street traffic the words barely registered. She caught up with him and fell in step. "Is it true that Mr. Lund is hurt?"

Even in a yellow blouse and long, brown skirt, Delia managed to look like somebody who had recently escaped from a convent. Wearing her hair in a bun didn't help, nor did the rimless spectacles she wore. Even in a ball gown and tiara, Delia would probably look as prim as she did now. But her earnestness made him smile. He liked her.

"The doc's taking care of him. He'll be all right."

They reached the café. "I could use a cup of coffee. How about you?"

"Well, I suppose it would be all right."

She sounded as if she'd been asked to have a night of wild, reckless sex.

A few minutes later they sat at a table with their coffees in front of them.

"Did either Carstairs or Norton ever get violent with her?"

"Norton did. Once. He slapped her. She had a bruise on her cheek. We had to work very hard to cover it up."

"Any idea why he slapped her?"

"He had the same one-track mind Carstairs did. He wanted her to leave Mr. Lund."

"And she wouldn't?"

Sweet little shoulder; sweet little shrug. "I think she might have. With either of them, actually. She was very bored. But they were too possessive. They'd get jealous of her being with Mr. Lund—her own husband."

"Was Lund like that with her?"

"Oh, no. She did what she wanted. And they'd get jealous of each other, too. She told me that Carstairs and Norton got into a physical fight over her. She thought it was funny."

126

"I take it you didn't."

"Of course not. I couldn't stand either of them."

"Did they know about Jim Holmes?"

"Alexis told me once that Carstairs made jokes about him. How pathetic he was and everything. You'd think that somebody with his—his short leg and all—would have more compassion. But neither Carstairs nor Norton is very nice. Not by my standards, anyway."

Her standards, Fargo thought. Those would probably reach all the way to the mountaintop.

"I need to ask you about the night in the hotel room."

"I told you what I know."

"I know. But I need to go over it one more time."

"All right. But I did tell the reverend I'd help him clean up his study this morning. He's not a very tidy man. And it will get my mind off poor Mr. Lund."

"Under oath you would swear that you heard all three of them in Alexis' room at different times?"

"Yes, I know their voices very well. Every time we'd come to town here they'd follow us around. They thought they were being very sly. That nobody would know what was going on. Even Mr. Holmes would do it. I felt sorry for him. He was just so sad about it all."

"But you didn't hear her scream or cry out or anything?"

"No. As I told you, I went down and got dinner. Then when I came back upstairs I found her."

"And you didn't see anybody in the hall?"

"No. I was with her so many years—I couldn't believe it when I saw her on the floor there. I just kept feeling for her pulse. But it didn't do any good, of course, not even when I started praying. I was crying all the time I was praying. I thought I was going to—be sick to my stomach, put it that way. But I wasn't. And then I went downstairs to tell the desk clerk about poor Alexis."

"You're leaving something out."

She blushed. "Mr. Lund didn't kill her."

"He was in the room."

"Yes, he was in the room. But he didn't kill her."

"You said yourself that you weren't in your room when she was killed."

"Yes. But he'd left by then."

"He could've come back."

"That's true. But so could one of the others."

Her small hands formed tiny fists. Her blue eyes blazed. "Mr. Lund did not kill Alexis and I darn well wish you would stop saying he did."

"I'm not saying it. I'm just asking questions."

"But obviously you're thinking it."

"No, I'm not. In fact, I'm sure he didn't. But in order to prove it I need to know everything I can."

The tiny fists unfurled. "Well, thank you for saying that. You could have said it when we first started talking and saved me a good deal of anxiety."

"Sorry."

She pushed her chair back. "I need to go help the reverend. He really is very untidy."

Fargo was walking up the steps of his hotel when a familiar face smiled at him from the doorway. Myrna, the waitress he'd had so much fun with the other day, caught up with him and said, "What a coincidence. I'm delivering a gift to somebody I know who's staying here."

"Anybody I know?"

"Could very well be. Maybe you should wait in your room and see what happens."

"That sounds like a good idea."

Even in a rundown hotel like this one, a certain amount of propriety was necessary. Even though the desk clerk would know that the fetching redhead Fargo had walked in with would wind up in his room, the woman would have to wait a few minutes in the lobby before going upstairs.

Fargo went into his room, got down to his long underwear. He'd left the door unlocked. Myrna pushed it open a bit later. Seeing Fargo sitting on the edge of the bed, she said: "Stay right there."

She closed the door behind her and then began to shed her clothes quickly. Her ivory skin and stray freckles were fascinating in the light. Even more fascinating was the way she brought her naked body over to him. Her hips moved knowingly, teasingly; the red hair between her legs was vivid against her flat, white belly.

Fargo was ready for her. She reached into his long johns and said, "Well, well. You're even bigger than you were the first time."

He laughed. "Practice."

She was already moist so she had no trouble opening herself to him and sliding down on his engorged shaft. "Oh, yes," she gasped. "This is what I was hoping for."

They began slowly, simply enjoying the first pleasure of their romp. His tongue found her breasts, his skill eliciting more and more small gasps from her as he focused on her nipples. He could feel her warm juices through the legs of his long johns. His hands began moving her up and down on him with greater force, and she responded by wrapping her arms around his neck and starting to put her hips to work. He could feel the muscles of her sex tighten sometimes to give him an extra measure of enjoyment.

Both of them lost count of how many times she reached her ultimate gratification. She rode him now as if she were bringing a fine horse across the finish line with a finale that would do each of them proud.

Toward the end, she managed to reach down and grab him, squeeze him. His entire body reared up. He got to his feet with her wrapped around him. He was still inside her when he deposited her on the bed. On top of her now, he began pounding them both to the final explosion of sheer breathless satisfaction. And when the end came, she held on to him, wanting to keep him intimate for a few minutes longer.

By then he was ready for more but she eased him off her, saying, "I've got to get back to work. Darn it."

He watched her get herself ready for the street. She moved with a simple grace that was beautiful to watch, her breasts rising as she slipped her arms into her blouse, her hips sensuous as they slipped into the long skirt she wore.

"I'll have to look you up more often," she said, smiling as she finished dressing. "I was going to the other night but the owner made me stay late because we had such 'important' customers. That's what he called them, anyway. They don't come into our place very often so he was impressed. But Norton kept grabbing me. He thinks women find him irresistible, apparently. I'm one who doesn't. Holmes and Carstairs were all right, though."

Fargo sat on the edge of the bed, rolling a smoke. He'd been concentrating on getting the roll just right, so at first her words didn't register. Then he said, "Those three were together? You mean the night Alexis Lund was killed?"

She thought a second. "Yes. Night before last. Why?"

"What time was this?"

"Around six o'clock."

"Do you remember if they all came in together?"

She came over and leaned down and kissed him on the mouth. "You're not very romantic afterward. All these questions. I was hoping you'd be setting something up for us later on."

He stood up, the lighted cigarette hanging from the corner of his mouth. His fingers reached it, set it down on the small table next to the bed. Then he swept her up into his arms and kissed her as if they were about to fall back into bed.

"Now that made me feel a whole lot better, Skye. But I'm still wondering why all the questions."

"Right now I can't tell you. But the next time we get together I'll explain it all to you."

"Will 'next time' be soon?"

"Soon as possible."

There in the sunlight she was a pure, proud, sexual woman. Plus he liked her. She was easygoing and fun in and out of bed. And she had given him a startling piece of information. What the hell had all three suspects been doing together right after Alexis had been murdered? They were supposed to be rivals, not buddies.

After she was gone, Fargo finished dressing and went over to the doctor's office.

Several patients sat in the outer area. The woman who ran the office was much more formidable looking than Dr. Standish himself. Her presence made it clear that no nonsense would be tolerated. The iron gray hair was matched by the iron gray eyes, and the stout body inside the green gingham dress foretold trouble for anybody who displeased it.

"I'd like to see Mr. Lund."

She shook her head. "Can't do it."

"I'm the one who brought him in."

"I guess you didn't hear me."

By now the coughers, wheezers, sneezers, and the others with various broken bones were all paying close attention. Fargo and the woman who ran the office were going to do them the favor of putting on a little show.

"I'd like to see the doctor."

"Can't."

"Why not?"

"Not here. Won't be back for half an hour."

"Is Serena here?"

"Asleep. All she's been through, I'm sure not going to wake her up."

"If you tell Mr. Lund I'm here, I'm sure he'll want to see me."

"Maybe so. But I don't plan to tell him. The doctor told me that he should get his rest."

"Don't try and talk Mae out of nothing, stranger," said a woman with her arm in a sling. "She'll just dig her heels in. Everybody knows that about Mae. The more you try and reason with her, the more she digs her heels in."

Mae smiled. "That's the truth, mister. Now you just be on your way."

Why couldn't Mae be a man? It'd be so easy just to knock him out and go see Lund.

The woman who'd spoken up was laughing. "She's got you now, mister. She gets everybody."

There was only one way to handle this and that was to rush past her and that was what Fargo did. With her angry shouts at his back, he hurried to let himself in the room where the doc had put Andrew Lund.

The medicine and some sleep had brought back some color to Lund's face, and his voice was steadier. "I see you met Mae."

"I'm hoping to take her to the dance."

Lund laughed, though it sounded as if doing so was a chore. "Believe it or not, they get a lot of unruly people coming in here. The doc needs somebody like her. I've seen her scare off some mighty big men."

Fargo walked over to the bed. Lund had been cleaned up and put in a fresh nightshirt. Three heavy blankets covered him. He was still pale but there was life in the blue eyes.

"Can you think of any reason that Carstairs, Norton, and Holmes would be hanging around with each other?"

"That sounds like a joke."

"Yeah, it does. But it isn't." He then went on to tell him what Myrna had told him about the other night. "All three of them were in her room at different times. And then they all end up together in the café."

From a side door, a voice said, "That doesn't make any sense at all." Serena came in, sleepy eyed, one side of her face striped with sleep wrinkles. She'd obviously been listening. "Carstairs and Norton hate each other. I don't know about Holmes."

"But they were together," Fargo said. "I trust the woman who told me about it."

A quizzical smile. "A woman? Anybody you'd care to mention?"

"Names don't matter."

"Maybe to me they do."

Lund laughed. "Been a long time since she had a man in her life. You'd better be careful, Skye." Then: "It felt good to laugh." Blunt fingers touched his head. "Every ten minutes I realize that this isn't a nightmare. It's real."

"I want to find out what they were doing together."

"That's for sure." Serena walked over to her father and began adjusting his blankets so that they covered him better. The room was lined with glass cabinets filled with medicines. The aroma was sharp but not unpleasant.

A shout; two shouts. The words muffled but the tone angry. Outside, in front of the doctor's office. Within moments something heavy smashed through one of the front windows.

Colt filling his hand, Fargo rushed out of the room and headed to the front. Even the formidable Mae seemed intimidated, as did the three women waiting with their children for the doctor. They'd huddled them all together for safety's sake.

Fargo didn't bother to look outside. He just strode to the front door, threw it open, and faced a group of about eight or nine men who were glaring at him. The one with two large rocks in his hands didn't bother to hide them.

"There's the gunny Lund hired," one of them said.

They didn't look like workingmen. Most likely they were drifting through town and decided to have themselves some fun. And most likely they'd been paid to have the fun. Somebody wanted trouble.

"You," Fargo said, "with the rocks."

"Yeah? What about them?"

"Throw 'em on the ground. The doc'll never get any money out of you for breaking his window. So I'm gonna take it out of your hide."

The thick, bald man in the sheepskin glanced at one

of his companions and winked. "I'll drop the rocks if you'll holster that gun, Fargo."

Fargo jammed the Colt back into its leather home. Then he moved toward the man. The bald one rushed him, and peripherally he saw another coming around the side of him. The bald one lashed out with a boot aimed at Fargo's groin. But he was too slow and too drunk to be any good at a move like that. Fargo grabbed his ankle and twisted his entire leg so that the man slammed facefirst into the street. Then Fargo brought an elbow up and over, colliding with the second man who was just preparing to jump him. He heard the satisfying sound of teeth breaking. The man's mouth bubbled with blood. Fargo grabbed him by the hair and brought his knee up and the man's face down. Now his smashed nose was bleeding as much as his mouth.

"Who paid you to come here?" Fargo said, shouting at the men who were too stunned to even run. It had all happened so damned fast.

He lunged at the bearded man closest to him. The man jumped back as if he'd been stabbed. Fargo pulled the Colt and put it in the man's face. "Who paid you to do this?"

The bearded one knew better than to lie. His eyes flicked around, meeting those of his friends. They gave him silent approval. "Sheriff Tyndale. We don't have nothin' agin the doc here or that Lund fella. We was just travelin' through."

"Yeah, well you keep on travelin' before you have some real bad luck like these two."

The injured ones were tending to their pain. In the case of the man with the broken teeth and nose, the pain must have been considerable.

Fargo might have felt sorry for him but anybody who'd hire out to smash up a doc's office didn't deserve his pity.

He flung the door to the sheriff's office inward with such force that the glass rattled in its frame. Tyndale didn't even have time to defend himself. Fargo lurched inside, grabbed Tyndale by his shirt, and slammed him against the wall. There was a part-time deputy in the office but Fargo didn't notice him. He didn't matter.

"You paid some men to start trouble at the doc's office."

"Fargo—I don't know what the hell you're talking about. I honestly don't."

"I know what you're up to, Tyndale. You want a lynching. Lund's got enough enemies that that won't be any trouble at all. Especially after sundown when you've got a good percentage of the population all liquored up. And you keeping them stirred up."

He let go of the lawman in disgust. He could see that Tyndale was embarrassed to be treated this way in front of his deputy. Deputies loved to tell tales and this news would be all over town within half an hour.

Tyndale did his best to look in charge again. He straightened shirt, vest, badge. He ran a hand through his thinning hair and pulled his trousers up. "And furthermore, you're damned lucky I don't arrest you right here on the spot, the way you busted in here. Karl over there could've coldcocked you any time I gave him the signal."

Karl, who looked to be all of twenty, nodded to Fargo. Apparently it hadn't occurred to him to coldcock Fargo, to sneak up behind him and lay his gun across the back of the Trailsman's skull. He'd been too dazzled by the sheer audacity of Fargo to do anything but stare in awe at what was happening. Imagine—somebody throwing the sheriff around the way this Fargo just had.

"I'm just an auxiliary deputy, Sheriff—remember that. My dad's the real deputy." Tyndale was going to raise hell with Karl for saying that after Fargo left. Here he was trying to portray Karl as this tough lawman who was up to taking on Fargo. Instead, Karl identified himself as green, timid, and pretty much useless. A kid who only got an auxiliary job because of his old man. Under other circumstances it would have been funny.

"You're trying to get an innocent man hanged, Tyndale. You don't have guts enough to do the job yourself so you're going to push it off on the townspeople. But it won't work. Because by nightfall I'm going to have your killer for you. And then I'm going to rip that badge off your chest and run you out of town."

Tyndale had to look strong in front of Karl. He tried but his voice was still shaky from getting pitched against the wall. "By nightfall, huh? Well, I guess we'll see about that, Fargo."

For the moment, anyway, Fargo had broken the man's spirit. Tyndale didn't even try to arrest him. But breaking a man's spirit could make him even more dangerous once he was able to get his bearings again.

There was nothing more to say. Fargo went back through the front door, slamming it so hard that the glass jiggled once again. He was glad for the cool air. He'd worked up an angry sweat.

Only after he'd walked for a time, his mind starting to relax, did he realize that it was three o'clock. He had approximately three hours to find the killer before Tyndale's lynch mob started forming.

15

There were two customers in the bank. The man was
flirting with a girl at a desk. The woman was re-
minding the teller that he was incompetent and insub-
ordinate. He managed to smile through it. He was
good at fake smiles. Fargo wondered how he'd be facing a firing squad. He could probably paste that smile
on even then.

He spotted James Holmes talking to his stern secretary. They both saw him at the same time. Holmes
made a sour face and took off at a half trot back to
his office. Fargo tried to follow him but his secretary
stood up and rushed over to block his way.

"You don't have an appointment."

"I have a feeling he'll see me."

"He can't see you. He's busy."

"Look at it this way. I know he doesn't want to see
me, but he'll have to see me. Otherwise I'll tell everybody in the bank here that he killed Alexis Lund."

Her lips parted in shock. "That's ridiculous."

"No, it isn't. And you probably know it isn't."

Just then he caught sight of James Holmes furtively
hurrying out the back door.

"Thanks for your time," Fargo said.

She started to speak but by the time she got a word
out, Fargo was at the front door. He needed to hurry
down the alley. Fargo didn't want Holmes to get away.

But as he reached the street and headed for the
alley, he started to think of a way that Holmes would

be more useful to him. If he just grabbed Holmes, he might not learn where the other two were. But if he followed him . . .

He slowed his walk, kept close to the storefronts, and moved behind a knot of people. Holmes appeared, looking a little frantic for one of the town's most important citizens. Fargo ducked his head. Holmes saw only the top of Fargo's hat and didn't recognize even that. And then desperately went on his way.

In a town the size of Reliance, shadowing Holmes didn't take all that long. After two blocks on the sidewalk, Holmes turned into a one-story, clapboard building with a discreet sign to the left of the door, NORTON ENTERPRISES. Fargo remembered being told that Brett Norton came into the office mainly to yell at people and impress himself with how important he was. Holmes glanced in both directions before entering. Fargo was still far enough back, still hiding in the midst of a crowd, that Holmes didn't even sense he was being followed at this point. Though that didn't seem to help his agitation or his nervousness any.

Fargo waited a few minutes before entering the Norton offices. He wanted to make sure that the men would be in a room they couldn't sneak out of. He walked around back. There was a rear entrance. He dragged a half dozen empty crates in front of the back door. This wouldn't stop anybody but it would certainly surprise them and slow them down.

He walked back to the front door and went inside. A young woman with dark hair and a pleasant, knowing smile assessed Fargo and obviously liked what she saw. "Good afternoon. May I help you?"

Fargo took off his hat and nodded to her. He wanted a quick survey of how the place was laid out. A narrow hallway led to the back where the offices would be. "I just got into town and I thought I'd surprise my old friend James Holmes. Somebody told me he might be here."

There were two risks here. She might already know

138

who Fargo was. And she might also question why he couldn't just wait till later to surprise his old friend.

"I was over at the bank and they said he came here."

She was as smart as she was attractive. She knew something was wrong. "Why don't you give me your name and I'll go tell him you're here?" She'd go warn them. She'd obviously figured out that Fargo was no friend.

He strode around her desk, moving well down the hall before she could even get up from her chair and chase him. The building was larger inside than he had expected. In the rear were three offices. Two of the doors were open. One was closed. The hushed male voices told him that this was where he needed to go.

"Stop! You can't go in there! Stop!" Her voice was urgent, strident in the silence.

By now she'd alerted the men. He yanked his Colt from its holster and hit the closed door hard with his shoulder. Then he was inside facing Holmes, Carstairs, and Norton. Norton looked to be scrambling for a desk drawer. Probably a gun in there. Fargo said: "Not worth dying for, Norton. Put your hands on the desk. Flat."

Norton scowled but did as he was told.

The secretary peeked in. "I'm so sorry, Brett." The familiar way she said "Brett" told Fargo that the girl had uses other than simply taking dictation. When Norton hired somebody he made sure to get his money's worth.

"Close the door, Nancy. I can handle this."

She didn't look sure that he could handle this at all. But she nodded and said, "All right, Brett. If you say so."

After the door was closed, Norton said, "Well, drifter, you wanted to talk to us. So start talking."

Carstairs and Holmes sat in front of the desk, Norton in an executive chair behind it.

"You're wrong about why I'm here, Norton. I didn't come to talk. I came to listen."

"What if we don't have much to say?"

"Well, I guess we'll all just sit here until you do. And when you talk, it'd better be the truth."

Norton sighed. He was an impressive sigher. The sound contained frustration, anger, contempt. "I suppose you want to talk about Alexis."

"You don't have to tell him a damn thing," Carstairs snapped.

Holmes said nothing. He kept his gaze on his folded hands in his lap.

"I'm not afraid to talk to him, Carstairs. There wasn't a damned thing wrong with what we did."

Carstairs muttered, "It still isn't any of his business."

Norton said, "You're seeing everything from Lund's point of view, Fargo. That puts you at a disadvantage. Lund's a little more complicated than you might think."

"I'm listening."

"Well, for one thing, he makes you bend to his will. And he puts you in your place—and he decides what that place is. He has more money than the three of us put together. And the same goes for his power. He's got important friends all over the Territory. We don't. So anytime he wants us to do something that's against our better interests—we do it anyway because he forces us to."

"I don't see what that's got to do with Alexis."

"It's got *everything* to do with Alexis," Carstairs said. "He finally met somebody he couldn't bully. She was as independent as he is and she wasn't afraid of him. I don't know if he knew about the three of us but after Alexis came he got worse and worse with us. He made us strike deals that hurt us in the long run—and made him even richer. If we didn't sign, he'd ruin us. And he made that very clear."

"You sure looked very friendly the night of his birthday."

Norton laughed angrily. "That was Alexis. Always

putting on the grand show. The grand front. She liked to have big parties. Any excuse would do. So we'd have to show up and pretend that we were happy to be there. While Andrew was bleeding us dry, making us sign on to business deals that didn't do much for us but did a hell of a lot for him."

"But you were all in love with Alexis."

"Love and hate," Carstairs said.

Norton said, "He's the philosopher. Or thinks he is."

"Well, how would you describe it then, Norton?"

Norton shrugged. "I guess you're right. Sometimes it was hard to tell if I hated her more than I loved her. In the long run I think she just used us to keep herself from being bored."

Fargo looked at each of them carefully. "And one of you killed her."

"Oh, hell," Carstairs said. "Why waste time?" He looked directly at Fargo. "We decided to force Alexis to come to a decision. Which one of us she really wanted."

Norton smirked. "She didn't want Holmes but since he was always hanging on her, we decided to include him."

"Include him in what?"

Carstairs said, "When we heard she was in a hotel room in town, we got together and decided to have it out with her. So we went over to the hotel together."

"And we each took turns going up to her room," Norton said. "And asking her to run away with us. We wanted to see if she'd actually do it. She'd led us on so long it was time to force a showdown. If nothing else, we'd have the pleasure of telling her what we thought of her. Which each of us did."

Holmes finally spoke. "Two of us sat in the lobby while one went up. None of us was up there very long. I guess Alexis thought it would be the same old thing. We'd be good little boys and not bother her with making any kind of commitment."

"She always got mad when you asked her for a commitment," Carstairs said. "She always said that it ruined the night."

Holmes flashed a bitter smile. "We really ruined that night. Three of us asking for a commitment."

"So which one of you murdered her?"

Norton sat back in his chair. "None of us. Andrew murdered her. None of us were up there longer than ten minutes each."

"Ten minutes is long enough to kill somebody."

"I suppose you're right. But we can each testify that we got the same treatment—Alexis mad at us, demanding that we leave. And we can vouch that none of us gave any sign that we'd killed anybody."

"We're not killers, Fargo," Holmes said. "If one of us had murdered her, we wouldn't have been able to hide it that well. We were each in the room about ten minutes and we came right back down to the lobby."

"You made a lot of noise while you were in the room."

Norton laughed. "That wasn't us. Alexis liked to throw things at you. Plus she was pretty good at shoving you into things. A very bad temper on her."

"But you loved her."

"I guess that's what it's called," Holmes said. "But I'm not sure. Even though I couldn't get her out of my mind—" He paused. "Even though she thought I was ridiculous—a part of me knew that I was addicted. Like opium or something. But the worst of it was I didn't like her. I saw her for what she was. I'm sure these other two gentlemen did, too."

Fargo could see Holmes as a pitiable figure. Extending pity to Norton and Carstairs was impossible.

"I knew I belonged at home with my wife," Holmes went on. "But no matter what I did, no matter how hard I tried to break away, I always went back to Alexis. Or tried to."

Carstairs said, "We didn't kill her, Fargo. Though God knows I thought about it from time to time. And I'm sure Norton here did, too."

"Ten times a day," Norton said.

This wasn't the time to make any final judgments but Fargo believed them. He'd come in here certain that one—or all three of them—had killed Alexis, but their story was just odd enough to be true. And in a strange sort of way, it made sense. The final confrontation of the spurned lovers against the evil-hearted enchantress.

"There'll probably be trouble tonight."

"If you mean a mob," Holmes said, "Tyndale had Pierce whipping them up the other day. One of my tellers told me that Pierce talked to a lot of miners about lynching Lund."

Fargo walked to the door.

"Where the hell're you going?" Carstairs said. "You haven't said if you believe what we told you."

"You're a big boy, Carstairs. Didn't your mom ever tell you about being patient?"

Before Fargo could turn the knob and walk out, Norton said: "None of us killed her, Fargo. But why don't you ask sweet little Serena about the time she pushed Alexis all the way down that long winding staircase of theirs? Serena hated her."

Fargo wished he hadn't heard that. He had no doubt it was true. But suddenly he had plenty of doubt about Serena's innocence.

As the mountains began to turn purple with shadow in the late afternoon, Fargo made the rounds of the saloons. Four were on Main Street. Two were near the wagon works. He could see that Deputy Pierce had done a good job setting everybody on edge. As soon as he pushed through the batwings, all the eyes fixed on him. Angrily. This was the man who'd thrown in with the killer Lund.

In each place, he said pretty much the same thing: "Most of you men have families and jobs. You don't want to lose them, especially when there's no reason to. You think that Lund killed his wife. I don't. But that doesn't matter now because he's in custody. He's also been hurt. He's not going anywhere. So there's no need for any kind of lynch mob. I don't have anything against you men and I sure hope I don't have to fight you. Don't let Tyndale use you this way. He doesn't give a damn what happens to you. He just wants to get even with Lund."

He got pretty much the expected response in each saloon. One man shouted: "You're workin' for Lund! You ain't worth listening to! We'll tear that doc's office apart if we have to." His friends got a good laugh out of that one.

"That's true. You can overrun us. A doctor's office wouldn't be much trouble for a mob to take. But I'll see to it that a good number of you die before any of us do. So I hope you stay clearheaded enough to think that through before you do anything stupid."

"He killed her and you know it!"

Fargo shook his head. "Right now I don't know who killed her. I need a little more time to figure that out. And when I know, I'll tell you. And I'll tell Tyndale, too. But for now I want to avoid anybody else getting killed."

There was no reason to say anything more. He turned and headed back to the street and the dying light.

They pushed furniture up against every door. They carried buckets of water inside to be ready in case the mob started hurling torches against the doc's house. Fargo had been able to line up four rifles in addition to his Henry. He made sure that each was oiled, loaded, ready. The doc and Serena were both decent shots—or so they claimed—so that would give them three shooters. Lund was too weak to shoot.

Summer dusks linger; spring dusks collapse into night almost immediately. The interior of the doc's office lay in shadow. Serena had cobbled together a meal of beef and bread and coffee. The three of them ate at a small table while Lund slept in the next room. Fargo talked but the words were automatic, almost as if somebody else was speaking them. He kept looking at Serena. She hadn't had an alibi for the night Alexis was killed. He'd ruled her in as a suspect, but then he'd ruled her out.

Now, given what Norton had told him about her getting violent with Alexis, he had to rule her back in for sure. When the doc excused himself to tend to Lund, Fargo said, "You told me you didn't get along with Alexis."

Her blue eyes gleamed in the stray starlight through a nearby window. She seemed puzzled. "That's right. And that's hardly a secret."

"But you didn't tell me that you'd once pushed her down a flight of stairs."

Serena had been about to take a sip from her coffee cup. The cup remained poised a few inches from her mouth. "Oh, God. Where did you pick that up?"

"Doesn't matter. What matters is if it's true."

She sat back in her chair. She surprised Fargo by sounding amused. "So I'm back to being suspect number one?"

"Not number one. I talked to Norton and Carstairs and Holmes. They claim they went together to force her to make a decision. They went up to her room one at a time that night. They're each other's alibis."

"And you believe them?"

"No. Not necessarily. There's even the possibility that all three of them killed her together. They were that frustrated over how she'd been treating them. So I haven't made up my mind about them yet."

"But you have made your mind up about me?" The humor in her voice was gone. A bitter tone had crept in.

"I'd just like you to tell me about it."

She took a deep drink of her coffee. "This got cold very fast." Then: "Whoever told you—and now I'm pretty sure it was one of her seedy boyfriends—only told you half the story. Alexis wanted me to give up my bedroom so she could turn it into a sitting room for herself. She said that there was plenty of room for

145

me elsewhere in the house. This was just one of her games to force my father to choose between us. She always had to feel reassured that she had all the power."

"So how did she get pushed down the stairs?"

Serena laughed. "She got pushed down the stairs, my dear, because we were standing at the top of the stairs, arguing. She pushed me and I pushed her back."

"And she fell down the stairs?"

"No. Not quite then. That happened when she tried to hit me. I believe it's called a roundhouse in fisti-cuffs. She swung with such force that when I ducked she lost her balance and went right down the stairs."

"Did you try to grab her?"

"It happened too fast." Then: "And to be honest, I'm not sure I would have even if I could have. I hated her, Skye. I've never tried to hide that from you. I despised her and there was nothing that could have changed my mind."

And that was when they heard the mob coming up the street.

16

They brought torches, guns, rifles, and plenty of
drunken anger. For some it was a lark. For others it
was a way of paying back a man they hated for numerous personal reasons. They numbered just above
twenty, the oldest in his seventies, the youngest six-
teen. There were two women, both older, both in man-
nish attire. When they reached the doctor's office, they
positioned themselves about fifteen yards from the
front door. A pair of them split off and worked their
way to the back of the place.

Fargo watched all this from where he was crouched
by one of the front windows.

The spokesman was a thickset man with a fierce
alcohol-blotched face and flashing dark eyes that probably looked just as crazy when he was sober. If he
was ever sober. He wore a black duster and carried a
Winchester. He stepped to the front of the crowd and
said in a surprisingly sane, businesslike manner: "There's
no sense in getting a lot of people killed here tonight,
Doc. There're too many of us to hold off for long.
Even with that gunslinger Fargo helping you out. We
don't have nothing against you, Doc. We just want
Lund. You know as well as we do that he killed his
wife. And you know as well as we do that with his kind
of money, he'll get away with it. All we want is to see
that he gets justice. So please don't make this any
tougher than it has to be. Just please open your front
door so we can see that there won't have to be no

fighting. Two of us'll come in and take Lund and then you can get on with your regular business. You understand what I'm saying, Doc?"

"His name's Nick LaPierre," Serena whispered from the window closest to Fargo's. "He used to work for my father until they caught him helping some rustlers steal some of our cattle. They wanted to hang him but he had two children so my father said to just let him go. And this is the thanks he gets." She almost choked on her rage and bitterness.

Fargo had raised the window three inches so he could rest his Henry on the frame, ready to fire. He said: "If Lund's guilty, he'll be charged by the law. All you're going to do tonight is get a lot of people killed. Tyndale's just using you and you don't even seem to know it."

"Tyndale don't matter to us. We got him and his deputy tied up back in his office. In case he changed his mind and turned against us if things got out of hand."

"Well, you're not getting Lund."

The crowd came alive then. Fists shook at the starry sky; curses came sharp as lashes of a whip; and a few of the drunker ones fired six-shooters into the darkness above. The torches showed frontier faces gleaming with beery bravado, eager for bloodshed.

The first shots came from the back of the crowd. They smashed the glass above the windows where Fargo and Serena crouched. LaPierre had to rush to the side of the crowd in order to avoid getting shot. Many of them were too drunk to notice that they just might kill their spokesman by accident.

Then shots exploded from a variety of guns and weapons. Glass shattered and the wooden front door was gouged again and again.

Doc Standish shouted from one of the back rooms, "You all right, you two?"

"We're fine," Fargo said. "But we'll have a hell of a time holding off this many of them for long."

Another volley of shots ripped and tore at the frame house once again. If they didn't burn it to the ground tonight, it was going to be an eyesore in the morning. Doc would be paying for a lot of repairs.

The first torch was thrown at the house a few minutes later. It landed on the front doorstep. The chilly wind kept it from doing any damage, thinning its flame and directing it away from the house. But there were several other torches and from past experience Fargo knew that fire would be most effective when the crowd got tired of shooting uselessly from far away and decided to rush the house in an attempt to grab Lund and drag him into the street.

Fargo knew that the crowd would soon tire of the standoff. They wanted to hang Lund. Then they wanted to get back to their saloons and brag about it. Drunk as they were, sloppy in their shooting as they were, Fargo and Serena couldn't hold them off much longer. At some point they'd be done in by the sheer number of would-be lynchers.

Then a smile briefly played on his lips. If it worked once, why not twice? There was no point in crouching here just waiting for the inevitable. If he could be quick enough, maybe he could turn the crowd back.

He whispered his plans to Serena. She still hadn't forgiven him for asking about Alexis falling down the stairs. "Well, according to you I'm this violent criminal, anyway. I guess I'll be able to hold off a few dozen drunks." She had her father's obstinate nature.

He made his way through the shadows to the back door. It took him several minutes to move aside the furniture they'd piled up there. He had to strain to move the five-foot storage unit. He could imagine the two men outside waiting to jump him. They'd be under the impression that he had no idea they were out there. He'd have to be careful.

When he'd cleared his course, he stood to the side of the door and opened it.

"Hey, that door's open," one of them said.

"Why doesn't he come out?"

"Maybe it just swung open by itself."

"Then what was he moving around in there?"

They were either more sober or more intelligent than Fargo had thought. He'd assumed they'd rush into the open doorway and he would knock them out as they crossed the threshold. Their caution irritated him. He was in a hurry.

But fortunately one of them just couldn't face the prospect of an open door without sneaking a peek inside. When he was two steps into the room Fargo jumped him and threw him back into his partner. He knocked him out before the man could even regain his footing from falling into his friend. And he knocked the friend out before he could set himself to throw a punch. They wouldn't be out long. More reason to hurry.

Fargo found the alley with no difficulty. He ran three-quarters of a block, then cut between two small buildings. He checked the street before he entered it. The mob was too busy shouting for Lund's head to notice a man behind it.

A big Vikinglike man stood somewhat back of the mob. This was the one Fargo would use.

Fargo hurried quietly up behind him and hit him with enough force on the back of the head to stagger him. The man fell forward. Fargo grabbed the man's hair and used it to drag him over to a hitching post. He took a rope from the saddle of a pinto that was tied there. He used the rope on the man's thick wrists, cinching him to the hitching post until he hung there, unconscious. Then he fired once into the air. Since no other guns were being fired at the moment, he got the crowd's attention.

They didn't turn toward him all at once. But all the mumbling and pointing finally got the entire mob to face him.

"He's got Lars!" somebody shouted.

Fargo put the barrel of his Colt to the right temple of Lars. "You've got two minutes to save your friend here. If you don't throw down your weapons and go back down the street to the saloons, I'll kill him. A lot of you think I'm a cold-blooded gunny. Well, unless you do just what I say, you're going to find out the hard way if it's true or not."

Lars groggily raised his head. He twisted around until he could see Fargo and Fargo's gun. "What the hell's goin' on?"

"He said he's gonna kill you unless we throw down our weapons," said a bald man in a deerskin jacket.

Lars, either because he was drunk or because Fargo's punch had rattled him, couldn't seem to comprehend what was going on. "What? How the hell'd I get tied up here?"

The man in the deerskin jacket repeated what he'd said.

This time Lars knew exactly what was going on. "He's Lund's gunny. Hell yes, he'll kill me. Now throw down those guns and I'll take care of this sunofabitch later. And don't try no funny stuff, neither. Lessen you want to get me killed."

"Guns and rifles on the ground, men," Fargo said.

The process began. Each man scowled and cursed and made a surly deal out of pitching his gun. The most popular line was "You'll regret this, gunny," followed closely by "This ain't over yet." Fargo had to stop himself from laughing. One man threw up. One man fell down. One man was so drunk he had a hard time getting his Colt out of its holster. A fine lot they were, a testament to lynch mobs across the land.

Even before they'd finished throwing all their guns to the ground, Serena came out, her rifle leading the way. She came over and stood next to Fargo. "You picked a good one for a hostage, Skye. You know who he is?"

"You can kiss my ass, Serena," Lars said.

"I take it you're not friends," Fargo said.

"He's one of the men who tried to steal my father's claim when Dad first came out here. He's hated Dad ever since." She smiled mischievously. "I was just sorry you didn't get to shoot him. Or at least beat him up a little."

"Bitch," Lars snarled.

Fargo untied him. Lars stood up, rubbing his wrists, swearing at both of them. "We'll be back."

"I doubt it," Fargo said. "You'll need guns and we'll have most of them hidden somewhere. You're already in enough trouble for tying up a lawman. That could send you to prison if Tyndale's mad enough."

"We were afraid he'd back down once we actually got our hands on Lund. He wouldn't go through with the lynching. He deserved to be tied up. Or worse."

"Nice bunch of folks you've got in this town, Serena," Fargo said.

He gave Lars a shove so hard that it pushed the big man three or four feet down the street. Fargo was sick of the sight of him.

Serena ran into the doc's office and found two large burlap bags. They collected the guns and rifles and went to see how Lund was doing.

"I almost feel sorry for Tyndale," Lund said. He was well enough now to sit up and sip broth from a cup without help. "He goes to the trouble of rounding up a mob and then the mob turns on him."

Fargo smiled. "Yep, if you can't trust a mob, who can you trust?"

Lund took some more broth and said, "This little room is getting to me, Skye. I just want to get home."

Fargo didn't blame him. The examination room was small and without windows. In effect it was a cell. "The doc tells me he'll let you travel the day after tomorrow."

Lund nodded then touched his head. "Still got the headache." Then: "Say, where's Serena?"

"She's helping the doc. They're whipping up your first meal. I think you might actually get some beef."

Fargo thought that might lighten Lund's mood but instead the older man stared into space and said, "I made a mess of it. Should never have married Alexis. Should have listened to all my friends. And to my daughter. But I knew better. That's one of my problems. I always know better than everybody else. I almost lost my daughter over it, and then I hurt somebody I didn't mean to, somebody I took advantage of."

"Is this the woman you mentioned that you'd been with once during your marriage?"

"Technically, once. Where we actually slept together. I was angry with Alexis and lonely the way she treated me."

The door opened and Serena came in bearing a small plate with half a slice of heavily buttered bread. "This is your treat for being such a good father."

Lund's eyes quickly glistened. He was weak not only physically but emotionally as well. Fargo considered everything the man had been through in recent days. He probably wouldn't have held up much better.

Serena carefully embraced Lund, not wanting to give him any additional pain. Then she took a knife and fork she'd concealed in her trousers and began to cut her father's bread. She obviously enjoyed feeding him.

Lund ate hungrily. Serena had to wipe his mouth twice because he wore a butter mustache. When the bread was gone, Lund said, "I don't suppose the doc would let me have the other half of that bread."

Serena kissed him tenderly on the forehead. "Well, if he won't, I will. I'm just so happy to see you eating real food."

When the door was closed, Fargo decided it was time to push for the answer he needed. He was almost afraid that he was right. But it was all starting to make crazy sense to him now.

"I need you to be honest with me," Fargo said.

"Why wouldn't I be?"

"About the woman you were seeing."

"Oh."

"I need to know."

After a time, Lund said, "I never should have done it. It was so damned selfish. It meant nothing to me and so much to her."

And then Fargo got the answer he was afraid he'd hear.

17

Main Street was emptying out for the night. Only the saloons vibrated with any kind of life. Storefronts looked dark and grim, the sidewalks shining with frost. The horses tied to hitching posts stood huddled against the cold. A church spire was outlined against the moon.

The hotel lobby was deserted. Not even a night clerk. Fargo went behind the counter, consulted the sheet that listed guests. Room 207. He was just closing the book when a wiry man with gaudy red arm garters appeared and said, "You ain't supposed to be behind there."

"That's right, I ain't. But you are."

"I was relieving myself. If it's any of your business."

"Does swiggin' down rotgut go along with relieving yourself? That stuff smells, mister."

He made his way up the stairs, not happy at all with what lay ahead. The hall was narrow, lit only by a single lamp on a table stationed at the far end. Fargo didn't hear the usual snores and grunts so he assumed that the place had a lot of empty rooms tonight.

He found 207, paused in front of it, and listened. A faint sound he couldn't recognize at first. Then—a rocking chair. Somehow that was right for her. A proper, prim young woman old before her time, suffocating under too many rules, afraid to live and enjoy herself because of an upbringing, Fargo suspected, that had ruined her before she'd had a chance.

"Delia?"

The rocking stopped.

"Delia. It's Fargo."

"Go away."

"I need to talk to you."

The rocking resumed.

"Delia. Lund died about twenty minutes ago."

A gasp, then a sob. "No!"

"Let me in, Delia. I want to talk to you."

"It's impossible. He can't be dead."

"He gave me a message for you right before he died."

He heard her get up from the chair. But she didn't come right to the door.

"Don't you want to hear what he said, Delia?"

She began weeping. As she crossed to the door she sounded as if she were dragging an enormous weight behind her. The door opened but he couldn't see her. He stepped inside. The air smelled of lilac water. The innocent kind a little girl would use.

He had to search the shadows for a glimpse of her. He took her into his arms and moved her over to the bed. At any other time she would have shrieked at the impropriety of sitting on the bed with a man.

"I lied to you, Delia."

She seemed not to hear at first. Then: "What? You lied?" Between gasps, sobs.

"He isn't dead."

"But why? Why would you lie?"

Then it was his turn to fall silent. Despite himself, he liked her, felt oddly protective of her. "I want to help you, Delia. So does Lund. We're going to get you an attorney from Denver. Lund's sure you won't spend much time in prison—if any. Especially if Alexis had the knife first and you were just wrestling with her and—"

"Please don't talk."

She stood up. Walked to the window with its frost and moonlight. Took a delicate handkerchief from under the left sleeve of her frock. She looked so young silhouetted against the window. She still gasped between words, though she was getting her weeping under control.

"Delia."

"I told her. That's what started it. I finally told her what I thought of her after all these years. I told her about my relationship with Mr. Lund, too. That's why she got so angry. Imagine. Here she slept with all these men but she went insane when I told her about myself and Mr. Lund."

Mr. Lund. A proper girl to the end. Not many women called their lovers "mister."

"She came at me with the knife. That's how it happened. We fell to the floor and"—she actually laughed—"I couldn't believe it, Mr. Fargo. She was jealous of me—jealous of me of all people. But I loved him and she didn't. And when I told her that, she said that I was insane. That he loved her and would always love her. She wanted every man on earth to love her. That's what it sounded like, anyway."

She walked over to the lamp on the bureau and turned up the light. Her small earnest face gleamed with tears. "I really didn't kill her, Mr. Fargo."

Fargo took her gently into his arms.

"A lot of people wouldn't blame you if you had."

LOOKING FORWARD!
The following is the opening section of the next novel in the exciting *Trailsman* series from Signet:

THE TRAILSMAN #324
CALIFORNIA CRACKDOWN

California, 1862—the death of a good friend at the hands of ruthless killers means that many will die before the Trailsman feels that his need for vengeance has been satisfied.

Skye Fargo eased silently from behind the tree and studied the two men crouched in the bushes ten paces from him. Both had Colts filling their hands.

Their intent was clearly the gold wagon coming down the trail toward Sacramento. And Fargo's business was to protect it.

Fargo knew there were three more gold rustlers on the other side of the wagon road that was the supply line up to Placerville and the mines in the area. It was also the only way to get the gold down to the banks and train lines in Sacramento. . . .

Cain Parker, owner of Sharon's Dream, one of the

bigger mines in the area, had begged Fargo to come help him protect his gold between the mine and Sacramento. Cain really didn't need to beg, since he and Fargo had known each other for years and had been back-to-back in their share of fights together. Fargo figured he owed Cain his life a few times over, so anything Cain asked, Fargo would do.

The name of the mine, Sharon's Dream, had come from Cain's late wife, one of the nicer women Fargo had ever met. She had always talked about she and Cain going farther west to search for gold, but it wasn't until after she died that Cain took his son, Daniel, then a teenager, and did just that.

Fargo had arrived at the Sharon's Dream gold mine a little after eight in the morning. The main house was a two-story wood building that looked like it would fit better just outside Boston. It was freshly painted white and stood out in the warm morning sun against the browns and grays of the dirt and rocks around it. Three long and low unpainted buildings near the edge of the hill looked like bunkhouses, one much larger than the others. The mine opening itself was about halfway up a rock-strewn hillside above and to the right of the bunkhouses, with the mine tailings spreading out below it like a woman's fan.

Placerville had started and gotten its name from an intense gold rush of Placer mining in the streams in the area. But as with most Placers, the gold had to come from somewhere, and soon the miners were digging into the hills, following the veins, or just digging in hopes to find a vein.

From what Fargo understood, Cain had managed to stake a claim to a really rich and long vein that so far showed no signs of playing out. He said it was taking almost thirty men to work the mine in shifts, cooks to keep them fed, and a number of hired guns to guard the place.

As Fargo rode up, Cain came running out of the house.

"Fargo, you old trail hand," Cain said, a huge smile on his face. "You are a sight for sore eyes."

"Didn't know you were having eye problems as well," Fargo said, climbing down from his big Ovaro and shaking his old friend's firm, solid hand. He had to admit, he had missed being around Cain. The two of them just seemed to fit together. Fargo knew a lot of people around the West, but he had very few close friends like Cain.

Cain stood about a fist shorter than Fargo, and was a good ten years older. But the age was only showing on his thinning hairline and the sun wrinkles on his face that disappeared completely when he smiled. The rest of him still looked as solid as a rock.

Cain could smile and laugh with the best of them. And he had the ability to inspire loyalty from those around him. Standing there with his old friend again brought back so many good memories of so many good times.

"How long has it been?" Cain asked, finally letting go of Fargo's hand.

"Too long. Four years, maybe five."

Cain laughed. "Yup, too long. How about we don't let that happen again?" He swung his arm wide, gesturing toward the spread around them. "So, what do you think of Sharon's Dream?"

"Big and impressive," Fargo said, telling the truth. "Sharon would have been proud."

Cain smiled at the memory of his wife. "Yeah, she would have been, wouldn't she?"

"No doubt."

Cain pointed up at the hill above the huge pile of tailings. "It's still pouring out the high-quality ore. In fact, we have a shipment headed to Sacramento today." He pointed to a wagon being loaded.

"Guess my timing is perfect," Fargo said.

"As always," Cain said. "You up for going to work?"

"No better time than the present," Fargo said.

Cain laughed. "I don't know. Some of my memories tell me the past was a pretty good time as well."

Cain introduced Fargo as the Trailsman to his six men that were to guard the shipment and made it clear that Fargo was in charge of getting the ore to the refinery, even though Cain himself was riding along. Not a one of them seemed to mind. In fact, most of them had heard of Fargo and looked downright relieved he was on the job.

He just hoped he could live up to whatever they had heard about him.

Fargo could tell that four of the men were hired trail hands and were comfortable with their guns. One carried Colts on both hips, and all of them had carbines in sheaths on their horses. The other two didn't look so trail experienced. One, Cain introduced as Hank, his mine foreman. The other was Walt, a young kid with strong-looking arms, a ready smile, and an eagerness to do anything to help.

Fargo had two of the experienced trail hands ride ahead of the wagon with carbines across their saddles, two behind, and Walt and Hank on the wagon. Cain was driving the wagon and Hank sat beside him. Walt sat on the gold boxes, riding backward to make sure no one came up behind them.

Cain said he had lost three good men so far in the last six shipments, but had managed to get the gold out every time. But the robbers had gained in number each time and it seemed like the focus was on Cain's shipments more than the other mines in the area.

Fargo didn't much like the sound of that. Sure, Cain was doing well, but if he really was being targeted, that meant there was a lot more behind this than just a gang of robbers taking opportunities as they came down the trail.

As they pulled onto the main Placerville road from the Sharon's Dream side road, Fargo had the wagon slow down. He wanted to give himself time to scout ahead on his big Ovaro stallion.

As the wagon moved slowly along, he was often a good distance from the road, moving along high ground to scout out what was ahead before circling back. He knew the Placerville road. He had been in the area a number of times as the gold boom exploded. With luck, he could clear this band of robbers out of the area in a few weeks, while enjoying some time with his old friend.

It was from a ridgeline to the north of the trail that he saw the five men taking up positions in a stand of tall trees and thick brush to ambush the gold shipment.

He had left his horse and moved silently down on them.

From the looks of the two men crouched in front of him, Cain had gotten Fargo on the job just in time. The wagon and the men guarding it didn't stand a chance against five guns blazing a short distance from the narrow corridor between the trees.

The two thieves were dressed like miners. They wore stained and faded overalls over dirty white undershirts, rough work boots, and thin-brimmed hats. These men were not professional robbers. They had been hired by someone to do this, which meant Cain had a much bigger problem than these five. This was no gang of trail thieves and gun sharps. This sounded like another mine owner with money who was after the gold ore coming out of Sharon's Dream.

The rumbling of the heavy wagon echoed ahead through the trees and brush and the two men both raised their guns, their attention completely on the road. With his Colt in hand, Fargo stepped toward them.

Fargo could move silently like a mountain lion when

161

he wanted to. He was within a step of the closest robber when the man glanced around and said, "What . . . ?"

It was his last word before Fargo smashed his fist into the man's face, the punch slamming him back into a boulder. The man slid down, unconscious.

"No!" Fargo said, pointing his Colt at the other man, who was just now turning to fire on Fargo.

Fargo put two bullets into the man's right shoulder. Fargo could see him teeter, then fall to the ground. But the man wasn't done yet. Lying flat on his back, he fired as he brought his gun up, his shot smashing wide and splattering into a tree behind Fargo. Fargo put two quick shots into the miner, then ducked behind a tree to make sure he was out of the way of fire coming from across the trail.

"Harry!" someone shouted from across the road. This one was hiding in a stand of trees about thirty paces away and slightly up the road toward the wagon.

It seemed that one of the two men had been named Harry. Fargo didn't much care which one. They had planned on bushwhacking and killing good men trying to do an honest day's work. They didn't even deserve names on the crosses over their graves. Actually, as far as Fargo was concerned, they were better served as buzzard meat.

One man eased out from behind a tree, glancing first up the road at the now stopped wagon and then over at where his friends were.

"Get back!" another robber said from his hiding place.

At least one of them had a slight bit of sense.

Taking no chances, Fargo aimed at the man who had left his cover and smashed his gun hand with a clean, quick shot. The man spun like he'd been dancing with a pretty girl in a saloon, then went over backward in a dance move no one would ever want to try to repeat.

Two guns opened up, splintering bark chest-high from the tree Fargo was using as a shield.

Fargo dropped to the ground, spotted where one gun was firing from, and patterned the area with three quick shots.

The shout of pain and then the sound of a body falling into the brush were clear as Fargo sat with his back against the tree and quickly reloaded all six cylinders.

For a moment, the forest was silent; then came the sound of a man crashing through the brush as the last ambusher ran for his life, trying to make it to where they had tied off their horses.

Fargo dashed across the road, his heavy boots pounding the dust.

Down the road he could see that Cain and his men had done exactly as he had told them to do when they heard gunfire. Cain had pulled the wagon off the road and into the closest shelter available. Everyone had dismounted and taken cover, their guns up and ready.

Up ahead of him, the ambusher was making a lot of noise as he scrambled up the open rock slope to the horses. Fargo burst out of the trees on the other side of the small grove just as the man worked to mount a reluctant steed. He also looked like a miner, but the horse and gear he rode didn't fit him.

And he clearly wasn't used to mounting and riding fast as he struggled to hold the horse still enough for him to get in the saddle.

Fargo took a deep breath. No point in killing him. Fargo almost smiled. The way the man was riding—looking like he was ready to fall off his horse—maybe he'd kill himself anyway. Carrying his Colt in a ready position, Fargo climbed up the hill the rest of the way to check on the remaining horses. They were well kept and the tack was expensive, the type you find the owner of a ranch using, not a fellow dressed like he was fresh out of a mine. Or, for that matter, the man down in the trees who looked like a typical rustler. Someone with money was behind this and had given them good horses for the job.

Marshal Tal Davis pushed his way through the batwings and strode into the saloon. He recognized just about everybody in the place.

He was looking for faces he *didn't* recognize. The burly, red-haired man behind the bar who went by the name of Irish was pouring a couple of miners rye when he glanced up and exchanged a familiar look with the lawman. Like all the bartenders in town, Irish was on notice to report any stranger who might be a hired gun. While paid killers didn't all look the same— nor were they the same in age or nationality—they tended to be cocky about their calling. Davis always laughed about how many hired guns got themselves killed in saloon shoot-outs by some local. It wasn't that the locals were so fast on the draw; it was simply that hired guns tended to have mouths as big as their reputations. They often got drunk and got into arguments that left them dead at the hands of a talented— and more sober—amateur.

Irish had sent a runner to tell the marshal that a suspicious-looking man was sitting in the back of the place playing poker and bullying the other four men sitting in.

A long bar of crude pine ran along the west wall. A small stage ran the length of the back wall. The tables filled up the eastern part of the place. A low fog of tobacco smoke hovered over everything.

Davis didn't have any trouble figuring out who the probable gunny was. At the moment the man was slamming his wide fist down against the table, making it dance, toppling poker chips. His harsh voice was made even harsher by his drunkenness and anger. "You think I don't know when a bunch of rubes are cheatin' me?" he said.

The other players watched in shock and fear as the gunny suddenly produced a shiny Colt .45 and pointed it at the face of a bald man.

"You been cheatin' me all along," the gunny said, "and now you're gonna pay."

"This is an honest game, Kelly," the bald man said. He managed to sound calm. "You're havin' a run of bad luck is all. And to be honest, it don't help that you managed to put away all them drinks while we've been playin'. Now my advice to you—"

"I don't want no advice from you!"

The few drinkers who hadn't been watching the card game now swung their attention to the man holding the gun on the cardplayers. They also paid attention to Davis. He now stood no more than six feet in back of the gunny, his own Colt drawn.

"I don't want trouble, mister. I'm the marshal here and as anybody'll tell you, I don't enjoy shootin' people. Now I just want you to turn around slow and easy and hand me your gun without me having to kill you to get it."

The gunny's shoulders and head jerked at Davis' words. His broad back, covered in an expensive white shirt—getting a better grade of gunnies in town, the lawman noted wryly—hunched some and his elbow rose. He was getting ready to turn on Davis and fire.

But the marshal, despite rheumatism, arthritis, and advancing age, moved with surprising speed. In four quick steps he was standing within inches of the gunny. Just as the man started to turn, Davis slammed his Colt into the back of the gunny's head. He was still a powerful man. The gunny stayed conscious long enough to spin half around. But by then the lawman's fist had exploded on the side of the man's face. The gun dropped to the floor and the man followed seconds later.

"We sure do appreciate it, Marshal," the bald cardplayer said. Even though he'd sounded calm when the gun was on him, his voice now sounded shaky. Sweat gleamed on his forehead. Sometimes a man didn't get scared until afterward.

"Just doin' my job, boys. But you could do me a favor by cartin' this one over to the jail and throwin' him into a cell. There'll be a deputy there to help you."

"Hell, yes, we will," the bald one said. He glanced down at the unconscious gunny. "Be our pleasure, matter of fact."

The other players voiced agreement.

Davis went back to the bar. Irish shoved a glass of beer at him.

"Thanks for letting me know about him," Davis said. "At least that's one less I have to worry about."

Irish scanned the place, making sure that business was getting back to normal. Didn't want to lose any money just because a gunny raised a little hell. Then his eyes returned to Davis. "It's the damned gold shipments. No easier way to make money than to hire some gunnies to hijack the gold."

"Yeah, and no easier way to take over somebody else's mine than by stealing all their profits." He took a deep swig of beer. Irish knew who he was talking about. Nothing more needed to be said.

"I'm your first stop?"

"Yep. Now I check out the other saloons and hotels. They're not all as cooperative as you. Easiest way to deal with gunnies is to get to them before they can do anything. But to do that I need people to keep an eye out. Most folks just don't want to be bothered."

"Or they're afraid."

Davis sighed. "Yeah, I guess I forgot about poor old Millard."

Ab Millard had run a saloon a block down Main Street. He'd sent a runner telling the lawman that a drifter who looked a lot like a gunny was doing some drinking and bragging in his saloon. Davis showed up and arrested the man without incident. He held him for five days, then sent him packing without any guns or weapons. Unfortunately, this particular gunny held a grudge. Three days after his release, now armed, he snuck back into town and killed poor Ab for cooperating with Davis.

"Glad you killed that little bastard when you caught him, Marshal," Irish said bitterly. "If you hadn't, I would've."

And Davis reckoned he would have at that.

No other series packs this much heat!

THE TRAILSMAN

**Available wherever books are sold or at
penguin.com**